RUTHLESS ELITES

ROYAL ELITE ACADEMY SERIES

M.A. LEE

CONTENTS

PROLOGUE

Micah

Confusion lines my young face as I stare out the window.

I know that I'm not supposed to be here—watching in the shadows—but I can't help myself. Chancing a glance back, I make sure no one spots me as I spy on the group of men who just pulled up in our driveway. My heart beats wildly in my chest, and my fingers trace the lines of frost on the cold, window I am still glued to.

A loud thud causes me to jump and I almost scream, but thankfully, I suck in my breath and remain quiet as a mouse. If my mom were to catch me... Well, I have no idea what she would do. I had been told since I was old enough to walk, not to look outside at night. I had always listened as the obedient child I was, but at some point, my own intrigue got the best of me. So, as I slowly slipped out of my bedroom and made my way toward the window at the bottom of our stairs, I knew that I would finally see what my parents had warned me about all of these years.

A scream pierces the night air and I see my dad, Ryder Lee, race around the front of my uncle Solly's SUV. My dad's strong features and dark hair make him look even more rugged and powerful under the light of the moon. He's my hero; strong and intimidating, but loving and gentle with his family. I watch my dad move with ease as he opens the passenger door. His face his void of emotion and I can't seem to tear my eyes away from him.

A man falls from the backseat, his hands and feet bound with rope. Even at the young age of nine, I know that he was hurt. A sliver of moonlight shines down on the scene, providing me just enough light to see his blood-stained face and clothes as he lay on the pavement.

My dad pulls out a pistol and my eyes widen.

So, it is true.

Kids at school used to taunt me, telling me that my dad was a mobster—a monster from the movies and stories only scene on television. I used to fight them, calling them all liars, but always knowing in the back of my young mind that their words were true. My dad came and went at all hours of the night and day. My mom owned a large Casino in Savannah, but I had heard enough quiet whispers behind closed doors to know that there was more going on, it was just that my young mind couldn't comprehend what it all meant.

Aiden Antoni and Chance Antoni, my other uncles, grabs the man by his throat and legs, throwing him into the trunk of his SUV. The men talk for a moment before they all jump into Aiden's SUV and drive away. I wonder if my family; Ason, Gabby, and Talon have ever seen their dads do something like this. We are a family, not by blood, but by loyalty. We spend our days together playing and they have been my family since the day I was born.

"Micah, what are you doing?" a familiar voice rings out from behind me. Only this voice is loud and frantic, a stark contrast to the sweet tone I usually hear.

Frozen in place, I don't dare to move as I hear my mom's chastising voice from the top of the stairs. She rushes down to me, spinning me around and holding me at arm's length.

Tears burn my eyes as I watch horror flick across her beautiful features. When I don't respond, she cries out again.

"Micah, what did you see?" she pleads with me. Her brows furrow and my pulse leaps.

"What was daddy doing?" I ask, my quiet voice dripping with confusion.

She looks at me and I see the pain behind her eyes. She thinks that I am scared. That what I witnessed terrified my little mind. Only, she's wrong. What I saw tonight only made me admire my dad and my uncles more.

The rumors were true.

My dad was part of the mafia.

He was a mobster.

A killer in his own right.

A smile spreads across my face and my mom's lips turn into a deep frown.

I wonder how many times she's seen bad things happen? I can't help but think to myself.

"Micah, your daddy was dealing with...something." She takes my hand and we sit on the bottom step together. I hear her sigh and I wait for her to finish talking. "Mommy and daddy love you so much. There are bad people in this world who want to hurt good people. Do you understand that?" she asks. I nod, praying for her to continue. "Your daddy and uncles—well—they stop bad people from hurting good people. Sometimes, they have to do things that may look bad, but it's for the best. I wish I could explain this to you better, but one day you will understand. Now, will you promise me that you won't tell anyone about what you saw tonight?" she pleads with me.

"I promise, mommy," I tell her.

And, I kept my promise for years until I was brought into the Antoni Mafia Family as a knight.

Chapter One

Micah

"Who wants another shot?"

I raise a bottle of Patron in the air and my red solo cup sloshes about. Everyone around me cheers and pumps their fists in the air as they all beg for me to pour more of the ridiculously expensive alcohol into their cups. My family's casino penthouse is filled with half of Savannah's most elite prep school kids and a few college kids who still come to one of the Elite's parties. And as one of the Elites, I know that anytime I throw a party, it's going to be a massive rager. You see, we are the Elite; a group of untouchable teenagers that have more power in one glance, than most of the adults in this city have. It isn't lost on me that most of the people at this part are only here for the free booze and a chance to say they were with the Elites in the infamous Old Savannah Casino and Hotel. None of us are really old enough to be in the casino, but when my mom and dad own the building that we are standing in, and my dad is a known member of the Antoni Mafia family—no one dares to tell me what to do.

A girl I recognize from my biology class slides up next to me, rubbing her ample breasts against my side as she flashes her long, fake lashes at me. I think her name is Brittany or Bethany or something that starts with a B.

"You want to take this party somewhere more private?" she asks, her warm breath a mixture of vodka and strawberry lip gloss.

I give her another glance as I take a shot of the Patron in my cup. I think I hooked up with her at the start of our senior year, but I honestly can't really be sure. Most of the girls at Royal Elite Academy look the same with their bleached blonde hair, fake tits that their rich daddies paid for, and enough make-up to keep Kylie Jenner in business for a lifetime.

There's a scowl on Talon's face as he watches me from the living room. His golden-brown hair and brown eyes make him look like a model, but his wide, muscled frame makes him the perfect linebacker for our school's football team. I feel a twinge in my chest, but quickly tame it down and ignore the feeling that comes from one of Talon's looks. Unfortunately, Talon never agrees with my antics at these parties. Don't get me wrong; he loves to have a good time, but I can sometimes push the limit. I can't help it; I like to have a good time.

And, Talon used to, too, until Ason left for college. Now, Talon has this weird fascination of being the mature leader that can keep the rest of us in control. Honestly, it's fucking hilarious. No one can control me.

"Move on, Amy," I hear Gabby say, as she steps up to us.

Damn, I wasn't even close to knowing this chicks name. I'm sandwiched between the two girls, but Gabby's presence alone could terrify even the bravest of men. I guess I should thank Gabby. Her fire red hair glows against the lights in the room and her green eyes give her an almost villainous look. Most girls are terrified of Gabby. Hell, most of the time I am, too. The girl can and has kicked my ass more times than I like to admit.

Amy stares blankly at Gabby, her mouth gaping open as she is unsure what to do next. While Gabby might not be a male, she is one of the toughest people I know. She's a great shot and will fight a bitch if she even dares to look at her sideways.

"Micah..." Amy goes to say something, but Gabby just reaches out and pulls her by her long, blonde hair.

"I believe I told you to leave," Gabby reminds her, shoving her away from the kitchen. "Besides, I doubt Micah wants to deal with chlamydia since you contracted it from Austin last week after the basketball game. Right? Or, is that just another rumor?" Gabby asks, narrowing her eyes at Amy.

Oh shit. Gabby is ruthless tonight.

Tears fill Amy's eyes as she rushes away. A group of girls who could be Amy's clone, follow after their friend. When I look back to Gabby, she's laughing at the sight and taking a sip of her own drink.

"Fuck, Gabby. You didn't have to cock block me," I say, smirking a little.

Rolling her eyes, Gabby slams her cup down onto the white Quartz countertop. "Please. I just saved you a case of the clap," Gabby sneers.

I can't help but laugh at that. "Well, then I guess I should thank you," I tell her.

Talon approaches and we stand in the kitchen, watching as the party continues on. Music blares loudly, but thankfully, we are on the top floor and there aren't any rooms around us. My parents are in Las Vegas for business, so I took the liberty of hosting a party here tonight. I don't live in the penthouse, but on a massive plantation near my uncle, Aiden Antoni. And the rest of the members of our family.

This penthouse used to belong to my mom before she married my dad. Now, it's available anytime I need a good time and away from the prying eyes of my aunts and uncles.

Talon offers me a cautionary glare as he glances all around us. His massive arms are almost bursting out of his t-shirt. Talon is the linebacker for our high school football team, and he is massive like a giant brick wall.

"So, how long until you start kicking some of these assholes out?" Talon asks me. "I see a few people I don't recognize," he offers.

Talons always too serious. If he would just lighten up, he wouldn't look like he is constantly in a pissed off mood.

"Do you want to me to take care of it?" Gabby asks.

Both Talon and I shout, "no," in unison. Gabby taking care of this situation could mean many things; shouting for everyone to get the fuck out, grabbing her glock and pistol whipping a few people, or making some people disappear.

"Nah, I think I am going to go for a swim," I yell, as I run past Talon and Gabby and make it out to the infinity pool. I've been standing for too long and my need to feel a rush is slowly creeping up on me. I've already had my dick sucked and taken shots while dancing with the hottest girls at school. I need something else to clear my head now.

***

An hour later and six more shots, I am buzzed, swimming in the infinity pool, and no longer bothered by Talon's angry stares.

I wish he would just leave, but I know better. Talon never takes me out of his sight. He doesn't trust me to not fuck up and Gabby... well, she knows that we are her brothers, and she would never leave us.

Naked girls swim around me and a few guys sit on the edge of the pool, watching with lust-filled eyes. To these guys, I'm a God and I fucking love how they all envy me. My head swims as I jump up onto the ledge. I'm off balance a little, but a great idea comes to my mind.

I move myself so that I am standing on the edge of the pool. Below me is a small balcony in case someone would ever fall over the side of the infinity pool. However, everyone around me is too drunk to notice, so I decide to mess with their heads a little.

As I stand on wobbly legs, I hear a few gasps from those around me.

"Micah, stop fucking around," Gabby yells out. She's sitting on one of the lounge chairs with Talon beside her. Neither one of them are amused by me right now.

"You could fall," a girl shrieks, her tits bobbing on the surface of the water.

Below me, I can see the city lights of Savannah and part of me wishes that I could just get lost down there. I make a scene of acting as though I'm losing my balance and then fall backward. I can hear everyone scream as they rush through the water to get to the side of the pool. When they look down and see me standing on the balcony below, their faces relax. Nervous laughter filters down to me. This is where I thrive. I've got them all where I want them. They never know what I am going to do next. Not only am I untouchable to them, but I am fucking nuts, too. And that is what gets me off—what drives the highs I crave so much.

"Ok, Micah. You've had your fun, get back up here now," Talon calls down from the railing next to the pool.

I should probably listen to him, but that's not my style. Instead, I move closer to the railing along the balcony, and I watch as Talon's eyes raise in concern.

"Micah, I'm not going to tell you again," Talon roars out.

Gabby rushes over to see what's going on and when she sees me hop onto the railing, I see a spark of fear ignite in her eyes. Unease grows in the pit of my stomach, but I ignore the feeling. I need to get that rush that puts me on a high that no drug can achieve.

Cars honk below me and now a huge crowd has gathered above me.

"Sorry, bro. I don't take well to orders," I call up to Micah.

Shaking his head, he curses, then turns and races away. I have no doubt that he is going to come down to this level and find a way to get to me. Gabby stares blankly at me; unsure of how to handle this situation. Unlike Talon, Gabby knows that the more I'm told not to do something, the more I want to push the boundaries. Her face hardens and I tense despite myself.

Everything begins to grow blurry from the alcohol I've consumed tonight. There's a nagging voice in my head telling me to get down, but it sounds too much like Talon to listen.

I sit on the railing, my back to the black night sky, and only the air surrounding me.

"Micah, come on up here," a brunette calls to me, but when I look up, her face is blurry.

Maybe I did have too much to drink.

"I'm just having some fun," I call out.

Suddenly, Micah storms through a glass door leading out onto the balcony and I lose my grip on the railing. My body begins to fall backward and my heart stills as a rush of wind smacks me in the face. My arms flair out in front of me and for a brief moment, I wonder if I've gone too far. It's hard to think when my mind is in a state of shock and my body doesn't seem to know what to do.

A firm grip reaches out and grabs me around the wrist, pulling me forward. Falling onto the concrete balcony, my body slams hard on the surface and a throbbing pain cut through me like a knife.

A laugh escapes me as Micah kicks me in the side. He's yelling at me, but I don't hear a word he's saying. All I can do is enjoy the last few seconds of my high before everything else comes crashing down on me. I may be an Elite, but I'm ruthless and nothing will ever change my wild streak.

CHAPTER TWO

MICAH

"Where are you going?" a voice asked from behind me.

I turn on my heel to spot Talon standing behind me, a serious look on his tense face. I know that Talon told Ason about my little stunt, and now I'm about to get my ass chewed out.

Anger courses through me.

Not this again.

Ever since Ason left for college and decided that he didn't want to be the Capo of the Antoni Mafia Family, Talon had been trying to step into the coveted role. However, what he was really doing was getting on my last damn nerve.

I knew that unlike Talon, Gabby, and Ason, I had more to prove to gain my role in the Antoni Mafia Family. Ason was the son of the Capo; his place was granted at birth. Talon was Chance Antoni's son and of course, he already had a place next to Ason. Gabby was Solly and Gia's son and she already had Antoni blood coursing through her veins. As for me, my father Ryder, had to fight his way into the mafia. One day, I would walk alongside them all and would do it still racing my bike and chasing highs. Because if I am being honest with myself, racing is what truly gives me pleasure. It's an incredible high that can only be found when you are driving at speeds that cause the world around you to fade away. Acting out and doing stunts like I did last night... well, that rush is short-lived. Racing, that is wild and dangerous, and I can never get enough of it.

Holding tightly to my bike—a Kawasaki Ninja 400, I push it out of my parent's massive four-car garage. It had been a Christmas present that I had begged my mom to get me. After I wrecked my Porsche, I was worried that they wouldn't get me another expensive and fast vehicle. Thankfully, I was wrong.

"Out," I say, trying to slip past him.

Talon slides over and blocks my path. His massive frame towers over me and his t-shirt looks like it is about to rip right off his large muscles. He knows exactly where I am going tonight and that is exactly why this whole song and dance routine is getting on my nerves.

Pinching the bridge of his nose, Talon releases a heavy breath. "Why are you so hell-bent on being an idiot?" Talon asks me. Leaning in closer so only I can hear what he is saying he adds, "Didn't you get enough adrenaline last night? That stupid fucking stunt could have killed you," he seethed.

I hate when he talks down to me. I'm a senior just like him, but Talon has always acted as though I needed someone to watch over me.

"I guess I just love watching you get angry. By the way, you look like the Incredible Hulk in that shirt," I laugh, pointing my index finger into his brick-like chest.

Talon lunges at me, but I side-step him and jump on my bike. He curses as I kick off the stand and start the engine. Even though we drive one another crazy, Talon and I are brothers. No one else in this world can insult us the way we can. We are family and that will never change—regardless of what any of us does.

And last night was just another reminder that no matter how many stupid things I do, he will always be there for me.

I drive off laughing, imagining Talon's red face as he watches my taillights disappear into the darkness. I enjoy the ride all the way to the fancy racetrack at the back of Will Zammer's property. Everyone at school knows that we love to race at midnight. None of us really race for money because we all already have that. Attending Royal Elite Academy in the heart of Savannah, Georgia, makes us royalty around town. Money isn't something we need, so we race for power and bragging rights. Though, sometimes, it does get old kicking all of their asses.

I zoom through traffic and only laugh when cars honk at me when I cut them off. Taking a sharp right, I drive down a one lane road until the only light is the moon above me. This is my favorite time to ride. The world around me is peaceful and for the time being, I am alone. When I finally reach Will's property, I can already see the glow of headlights and the roar of engines. My peace is gone, but I am about to experience a new kind of euphoria.

Racing.

As I pull up to the rest of the racers, the crowd that has gathered watches me. I feel their eyes boring into my soul and the excitement of the power in their jealousy only fuels my adrenaline more. While we are all wealthy, they all know that I have something none of them will ever have. I have the mafia on my side. I have a deadly power and prestige their family's wealth just can't buy.

That's just another one of the reasons I love racing. When I put on my helmet, I can block out the rest of the world. It's just me and the road.

I pull up to the starting line and then hop off my bike. I spot Will sitting in a fold-out chair and his wide grin tells me that he's already buzzed. He pulls a joint to his lips and takes a heavy puff.

"Micah Lee. I didn't think I'd see you here again," he says slowly.

A few people eye me, but no one dares to say anything. They are too busy entering the names on our private social media group where we get the race details and locations. All racers have to comment they are going to race so they can get qualified.

Shaking my head, I narrow my eyes at him. "Why wouldn't I be back?" I question.

Leaning down, I take the joint from his hand and bring the weed up to my lips. I take in a draw and then exhale the smoke in a large puff.

"Just thought you got your kicks already. But no worries. Join the race and let's get this shit started." Will claps, stealing his joint back.

Laughing, I shake my head as I turn and make my way back toward my bike. "No way, man. There isn't a high I won't chase," I shout over my shoulder.

When the race begins, I don't hesitate to rev my engine and push my accelerator as far as it will go. My bike jumps, but it moves with ease through the freshly paved track. The other racers keep up with me, but none dare to try and pass me—even though I know their bikes have just as much power and speed as mine does. A spark of anger flares inside of me and I roar out a curse. Why won't they try and pass me?

I want them to push me to the limit. I need competition; to feel adrenaline course through my veins at the thought of someone beating me. To give me a reason to push myself and my bike harder and faster. Wind rushes all around me as I glance side-to-side at my opponents. When I cross the finish line, I don't get the rush I had been chasing after.

And now, I'm fucking enraged.

A few guys come up and congratulate me, but their words are fake. They let me win because I'm part of the Elite. I'm a god to them and you don't show up a god. Pissed off, I kick my bike and watch as it falls over and slams onto the ground.

"Damn, what's wrong with you?" Will asks me.

His eyes are blood-shot red, and he's got one of the cheer-leading captains hanging off his arm. She's just as high as he is.

"I'm tired of these shitty races. I need something with more—competition," I announce, glaring at the guys who are now slinking away from me.

Will nods. "You should check out the races on the north side. Money isn't as much, but the racers are wild, and they never get broken up by cops. Only thing, it's a pretty rough part of town."

I think this over for a second. Maybe this may be the next step I need to take.

"I'm in," I say, slapping him on the back.

CHAPTER THREE

STELLA

I grip the sheet tighter around me as I watch the morning sunlight filter through the dirty blinds.

A heavy ball settles in the pit of my stomach as I am reminded that it is the first of the month.

Bills are due.

Rent needed to be paid, and my mom had been on another month-long bender, and I was sure that the little money she had received from her government assistance was long gone.

The sound of a car backfiring and dogs barking echoed through the thin, trailer walls. I really hated it here.

My alarm blared, another reminder that a new day was starting, and I was still trapped in this endless cycle of shit. Throwing the sheets off of me, I get out of bed and pad across the dingy floor of my small bedroom. After a cold shower, I dress in a pair of tight jeans and the only clean t-shirt I could find. By the time I walked out of the trailer, my best friend, Ally, was already waiting outside for me.

Her neon green Jeep was about twenty-years-old and sounded like it would blow up if she pushed the accelerator too far. It was her dads, before he was killed a few years ago in a convenience store robbery. Now, she drove us to school, while her mom entertained men to pay the bills.

We were trash.

Discarded and looked down upon because we didn't have money like the elite members of the Savannah Proper Society. As I moved toward her Jeep, I stopped and pulled up the tarp I had thrown over the motorcycle I kept hidden near the trash cans. No one knew it was there, and I felt a spark of excitement course through my veins at the thought.

Glancing back at the door, I spotted the notice from our landlord taped to the front door. We were already behind from last month and I didn't have the money yet. Ripping the paper from the door, I crumpled it in my hand and threw it on the rotting front steps.

"Hey," Ally called, as I jumped into the Jeep.

"Hey," I acknowledged, as I nestled into the worn, passenger seat.

"Rough morning?" she asked, giving me a glance.

"You could say that," I grumble.

Ally always knew when to shut up, and I loved that about her. We both knew that sometimes, talking about what was bothering us was worse than the problem itself.

We drove through town as we made our way toward Carver Heights High School. When people thought of Savannah, Georgia, they typically imagined the lush Spanish Moss trees, romantic historic districts, and coble stone streets. What they didn't envision were the dirty streets with rundown homes. We made up the part of Savannah that wasn't glamorous and romantic. The north- west side of Savannah is where I live and where tourists and the rich never venture down to. The southeast part of Savannah is where most of the wealthy live. We pass by the sign for Carver Heights, one of the crime capitals of Savannah, and where I live.

Even the damn city sign looks depressing with its worn wood and paint-chipped letters.

Ally turns up the music and rolls down the windows, allowing the soft, gentle breeze to race through my long, blonde hair. The air conditioner wasn't working in the trailer and the muggy nights were almost unbearable. I needed to make some money soon so I could pay to have it repaired. I had no idea when my mom would come home and without a dad, I was on my own.

To be honest, I preferred it that way.

I chewed on my fingernail and Ally quickly glanced my way. "What's wrong?" she asked, as she ran a hand through her brown hair. I guess she finally decided to check in on me. I wasn't usually this silent and I could tell that she was worried.

Ally could always tell when I was anxious or stressed. We had been friends since we were five-years-old when we met in the center of the street of the trailer park. No one cared to watch us, so we began to watch out for one another. She was the only one who truly understood what it was like to live like scrum.

"I'm almost out of money," I sighed.

"Do you have another race coming up?" she asked, her tone lowering.

Ally hated that I raced my motorcycle for money. She thought it was reckless and dangerous. While she wasn't wrong, it was the only way that I was guaranteed quick cash unless I planned on stripping—which was completely out of the question.

Sadly, most girls where we live end up stripping at the local strip clubs, or hustling on the streets. Those were ideas I was willing to entertain. Regardless of where I came from, I wanted more out of life than this.

Thankfully, one of my mom's old boyfriends had left his bike after he had been arrested and she kicked him out. To be honest, he wasn't a bad guy. His name was Matt, and he had been the first boyfriend of moms that was decent and didn't try to hit on me. He taught me how to ride the bike and always kept food in the house. Though, when he got arrested for dealing drugs, he left, and I never saw him again. I had originally thought about selling the thing for parts, but

I decided against it. I continued to teach myself how to ride the bike, and then realized that not only did I enjoy riding the bike, but I had found illegal races nearby where I could make money. My neighbor, Johnny, was talking about it one night and I had listened intently to his conversation. At first, when I had entered, guys laughed at me and didn't take me seriously. However, after I beat them all, they started allowing me to race against them. Now, I was making enough money to cover rent and other bills, too.

Ally had managed to get a job waiting tables at a small diner near where we lived. She earned barely enough tips to buy groceries, but at least her mom made sure the main bills were paid. I wasn't that lucky.

I'm on my own.

Nodding, I stare out the window, watching as we pass by the old, run-down buildings that line the dirty streets. Up ahead, I can see the skyline of downtown Savannah and for just a brief moment, I am given hope that maybe one day, I won't be stuck on this ugly side forever.

"Yeah, but I heard some new guy entered the race. Some rich guy with a fancy bike. I just had to add a new part to my bike, and I really can't afford to lose," I say.

Worry causes a lump to form in my stomach. I quietly wonder what it would be like to not have to worry about paying bills or which creep boyfriend my mom will come home with next time.

"Why don't you just come work with me at the diner?" Ally asks, though she already knows I'm going to turn it down.

Shaking my head, I glance at myself in the side mirror. My green eyes look almost sunken in and my hair is messy in a high ponytail. "I would never make the kind of money that I need," I explain. "At least with racing, I know how much I will take home if I win. With waiting tables, I have no way of knowing what I would make each night."

The thought of being kicked out of my tiny trailer—though it is disgusting and in major need of repairs—is still a daunting feeling. I would have nowhere to go.

Ally pulls up to our school parking lot and I see the police already making their rounds on the school campus. It's not uncommon for a fight to break out or a drug bust to happen before our first period of the day. As we walk across the lot, I suck in a deep breath. Other than racing, school is my only other chance at freedom. Maintaining good grades has put me on track to apply for college scholarships for next year. Most seniors here could care less about their futures. They know that they will end up at some dead-end job just like their own parents. But for me, I can't allow that to become my fate. I want more for myself than becoming just another statistic that people pity and look down upon.

Walking into school, I ignore the loud sounds of students in the halls talking and slamming locker doors. All I can think about is my upcoming race and how I can escape this reality.

Chapter Four

Micah

"Hey, are you going to be slumming it again tonight?" Talon asks, as he eyes me carefully.

Ason and Scarlette sit on the back porch, holding hands and looking too cheesy for my taste. They are in town for the weekend, visiting from college. Ason had some business to help take care of as the Antoni Mafia Family was venturing into an entirely different world—owning a bakery. Apparently, Ason's now fiancé, Scarlette, has a thing for sweets, so they are opening a small bakery just outside of Savannah.

"Nah man, I wasn't planning on taking out any of your girls," I joke back.

Talon rolls his eyes at me, but I can see him try and hide a chuckle. This is just what we do—we banter back and forth. Sometimes we even fight, but at the end of the day, we are brothers, and we would do anything for the one other.

"Listen, we have a meeting tonight. You have to be there," Talon reminds me.

Nodding my head, I straddle my bike and put my black helmet over my head. "I know. I am just going to fill my bike up with gas and then come back. My race isn't until midnight," I remind him.

What I don't tell him is that I am moving to a different track tonight. At my last race, I heard some guys talking about an illegal track down by the old warehouse district. The place had been abandoned for years and only housed trash and the homeless. It was the perfect place for illegal racing as no one ever dared to venture down that way—even the police. If I let any of the guys get wind of what I was doing, they would try and stop me.

"Hey, Micah," Ason yells, as I kick off the stand.

I turn to face him and see the seriousness on his face. "Yeah."

"Don't do anything too stupid," he yells.

Ason was the first person I told when I started racing. He wasn't happy with me, but he wasn't surprised either. I've always had a streak for doing things a little...wild. Ason promised that he would keep everyone off my back as long as I promised to be safe. So far, I had done just that.

"I wouldn't dream of it," I say, smirking as I take off down the long driveway.

As I begin to drive, I pass by Gabby as she enters the property. Her red hair dances around her face as her window is rolled down, allowing wind to rush inside the car. She offers a wave, but doesn't stop. She's been pretty quiet lately, so I make a mental note to remember to ask her what's up later.

Driving through the streets, I take in everything as I make my way to the gas station. After filling up my bike, I make it back to the house where everyone is now settled inside. I spot my dad standing next to Aiden, Solly, Chance, and Gabby's mom, Gia. They are talking in hushed voices, but when they notice me walking through front door, they all stop and stare at me.

"What?" I ask, not liking the way silence has filled the area.

"You are five minutes late," my dad warns.

To be honest, I hadn't been too concerned with the time. I didn't think I'd been late, though. Now I knew I had pissed everyone off.

"Sorry, I guess I lost track of time," I stated.

Everyone turned and walked into the large dining room where Gabby, Talon, and Ason were already seated around the table. No one spoke until I was seated, which made me nervous. The vibe of the room had shifted, and I felt tense and uneasy.

"Now that everyone is here, we can begin," Aiden says, glaring daggers my way.

As our capo, Aiden is the one we all answer to. Upsetting him could literally be a life-or-death situation. Knowing I'm in trouble only sparks more frustration inside of me.

"Ason is in town this weekend to discuss a few new business ventures we are partaking in," Ason continues. "I am looking at each of you to take on another venture," he says, eyeing each of us kids carefully. I gulp as his eyes linger on me. "I need to trust that who I pick for this role is smart, logical, and has a primary focus on the Antoni Mafia Family name," he finishes.

My dad nods as Ason looks to him. "We are looking at creating another casino and hotel near Atlanta. This one would be more for the high rollers and people who want to enjoy the life of luxury, but without the nonsense of the general public," he says.

What he really means is they want to cater to the super wealthy; celebrities, politicians, and mafia. People who don't want to be seen and want all of their dirty secrets kept hidden, but for a cost, of course.

"Talon has already shown an interest in this, but this will take two of our men to run successfully," Chance speaks up.

"Gabby already has stated that she wants to work closely with her mother and run intel with our gun shipments," Solly says, looking over to his daughter adoringly.

Listening to them speak, I know that they are looking for Talon and I to take this on, but I see the worry laced in their features. They don't trust me. A pit forms in my stomach, but I try to hide any worry that I may feel. I guess I will just have to prove to them that I am worthy of this.

"Talon and Micah," Ason begins, turning in his chair to face us, "You two need to start thinking about your future and how you are going to carry on our legacy."

All I can do is nod and Talon does the same. My life revolves around the mafia, and I know that one day I will have my place with the made men. But for now, I want to enjoy my last few years of freedom—or as close to freedom a guy like me can get. The tension in the room is so thick you could cut it with a knife. Ason and Talon expect me to be in the mafia mindset already. In some ways I am, but mostly, I just want to race my bike and have fun. In due time I will be faced with the evils and seriousness of the world. Until then, I just want to live my life.

"We know what we need to do," Talon speaks up.

The meeting continues, but I drown out all of the chatter. All I can think about right now is getting back on my bike and enjoying a late-night ride.

CHAPTER FIVE

STELLA

"Hey, rent was due two weeks ago."

Cringing, I turn as I hear the deep, throaty voice call out to me. Slowly turning, I spot Lucas, our overweight and sweaty manager of the trailer park. His eyes drink me in that creepy way that lets me know he is thinking something awful. He knows I am a minor, but guys like Lucas don't really care about that.

"Yeah, I will have it to you by tomorrow," I say, trying to plaster on a fake smile.

Several women around here have traded other favors to Lucas when they didn't have enough money to cover the rent, but I just can't bring myself to that. Stooping that low isn't my style and I want to get out of this place one day.

The harsh light of the dingy streetlamp glows around us, and I listen as the sounds of buzzing mosquitos hum through the air. Sweat slides down his greasy forehead as he licks his lips. My stomach drops and I want to puke right on the spot.

"That's what you said last week," he states, kicking up dirt and gravel as he makes his way over to me.

A cigarette hangs out of his mouth and the smoke billows around us as he nears me. I quickly check the time on my phone and realize I only have a few minutes until the race begins. I will be late and won't get my name entered if I don't leave now.

"I swear, you will have it tomorrow," I fumble out, taking a step back. My bike is still hidden under a tarp behind the trailer, and I need to get to it now.

Lucas sneers as a wicked smile grows on his face. "How about we talk about other ways that I can collect my money," he proposes, causing bile to rise up in my throat.

I can smell the stench of sweat mixed with stale cigarettes. I can barely muster my next words as fight back the gagging sensation. "Lucas, I am going right now to collect my money. I will leave it in the mailbox first thing in the morning," I tell him.

I can't stand here any longer. I turn to leave, but Lucas reaches out and grabs my arm, stopping me from escaping. His grip on my arm tightens and I feel panic rising inside of me. There is no use screaming for help. Out here, people yell, scream, and cry at all times of the day and night. The pleas just go ignored because getting involved could be deadly.

"I know you think you are smart, but you and your whore mother are about to get kicked out of here if I don't get what I want, I will have to find other ways to be satisfied." His grimy hands still hold onto my arm.

I try to squirm out of his hold, but he only digs his dirty fingernails deeper into my skin. His hot breath reaches the back of my neck and that's when I finally feel my anger and fear grow into a toxic storm. Using my other hand, I shove him away, causing Lucas to stumble back a little.

"You little..." I don't hear the rest of his insult as I race around the corner of the trailer and jump on my bike. As the engine roars to life, I hear Lucas running toward me. I kick off and begin driving out of the trailer park. The wind from the drive attempts to cool my down, but face is flushed with heat, and I hate how my life revolves around threats and worry. One day, I swear I will get myself the hell out of here.

***

I make it to the track just as Tank, the guy in charge of assigning the racing spots and collecting the bets, begins shouting orders. I see a large crowd forming behind the old, abandoned warehouse and I slowly pull next to a few other bikes. People stand around, drinking and smoking as they place their bets. A few girls strut by in short skirts and low tops, and I watch as the racers eye them with lust-filled eyes. Thankfully, my helmet is still on and covering my face. My black leather jacket hugs my frame and hides my breasts. Most people here know that I am a girl, but I heard there were a few new drivers tonight, and I didn't want them to see that I was female.

I park my bike at the starting line and make my way over to Tank. His large frame towers over everyone else as he takes money and names down on his phone.

"Name?" he asks, as I approach him.

"Stella," I say in a low voice.

Tank nods his head and jots my name down. Tank is a pretty decent guy. He doesn't ever out me to the new drivers and doesn't make a big deal out of a girl racing with guys.

After everyone has been entered, we all move back to our bikes and get ready for the race. The crowd clears around the track, standing close by so they can see all of the action firsthand. The track goes through the old warehouse district and has some pretty sharp turns and slick spots from years of unuse. I straddle my bike, watching as a guy I don't recognize idles up next to me. Blonde, disheveled hair hangs over the guy's blue eyes and as he goes to place his shiny red helmet over his head, it's then that I notice there's more to this guy then his insanely good looks.

He's driving one of those super expensive racing bikes. Why would anyone who could afford a bike like that, be down here on the rough side of Savannah? Noticing my staring, the guy turns and gives me a once over. I'm grateful that he can't see inside my mask; because he would see my red cheeks and eyes that are drinking in him. My heart flutters and I have to push down that feeling. I am here to earn money. I can't let some hot guy—wow, he is scorching hot—to distract me.

"You got a staring problem?" the guy growls out, causing me to lose focus for a moment.

He shakes his head and lets out a laugh before revving the engine on his bike. Damn, I have to clear my head, or this guy will cause me to lose the race. I focus my attention on the track ahead as a girl in a black and white plaid skirt and hot pink bikini top struts onto the track. She holds up a checkered flag and the crowd hushes. All I can hear are the engines purring and the sound of my own beating heart. I have so much at stake here.

"Man, I hate it when those rich kids come down here to our races," a guy beside me bellows out.

He is staring daggers at the guy on the other side of me and I can't help but feel the same way, too. Rich kids have no idea what it's like to have to fight for what we have. They don't understand the fear of not knowing how you are going to pay your bills or where you will sleep that night. They think this is all fun and games—a joke. However, for kids like us, this is survival.

I'm so lost in my own anger, that I almost miss it when the girl standing in front of us drops the checkered flag and announces the start of the race. I'm late kicking into gear and I know that slight mishap will cost me in this race. I launch my bike forward, driving as fast as I can while maneuvering through the broken asphalt of the track. My bike rattles a bit, but it holds up nicely as I make the first sharp turn around an old warehouse that was once used for shipping containers. I speed past a few guys, and I feel my own high starting to build. This is why I love racing. The suspense is wild and always makes me feel so alive.

The rich asshole is only a few feet ahead of me, but right now, it feels like he is miles away. Anxiety creeps in as I start to really worry that I could lose this race. If I can't pay Lucas, the owed rent in the morning... I can't even think about what will happen. I have no idea where mom is right now. She's probably strung out on heroine at her latest boyfriend's place. Her cell phone was disconnected a week ago, so I really have no way of getting ahold of her. That thought, plus my own growing worry, causes me to push the accelerator down harder. I feel my bike jump a little as I push it harder than I ever have before. I speed past a few more racers, but as I see the finish line up ahead, the crowd is cheering, but I realize instantly that it's not me who they are yelling for.

The rich asshole makes his way across the line and dread finally consumes me. I slow my speed as I make my way to the line. People crowd around him, and I fight back the hot tears that threaten to spill down my face. I hate crying—it's such a vulnerable emotion and I refuse to allow these people to see me cry. Shaking with rage, I hop off my bike and run over to the guy as he pulls off his helmet. A few scantily clad girls rush him, but I shove each of them out of my way.

"Hey," one girl cries out, as she stumbles on her heels.

"Move, bitch," I roar, and her friends quickly jump out of my way.

The guy turns and spots me, giving me a serious look. "Whoa, calm down, man," he says, offering a slight chuckle. "You can't win them all," he jests.

I reach out and shove him in his rock-hard chest. Of course, he has a solid wall of muscle that feel chiseled like he's some Greek god brought down to earth. I loathe him already.

Tearing off my helmet, I allow my long, blonde hair to fall out of the messy ponytail I had tucked it in. The guy's eyes go wide as he realizes that I am a girl. More people begin to crowd around us, waiting and watching to see what happens next. This isn't the first time that I have swung on a guy, but never has some wealthy prick from the nicer part of Savannah ever ventured down to our turf.

"What the hell?" he asks, taking a step back.

He seems unfazed by my shove, but seeing as he is nothing more than muscle, that is to be expected.

"Do you think this is some type of joke?" I scream out to him.

"Hey, Stella. Calm down," I hear Tank yell, as he walks over to us.

He's holding a stack of money in his hand, and I wince as I think about how that was supposed to be my earnings tonight.

A few guys around us chuckle and whistle, but none dare to intervene. They know that I don't put up with their shit.

"What is your problem?" the guy asks again. He licks his lips as he looks me up and down.

"My problem?" I roar out, throwing my hands up in the air. "You don't belong here. That money should be mine," I state angrily.

The guy laughs and his hair bounces around his face. "Last I checked, this was a free country. I came here to race just like you did. Don't be angry that the better man...I mean person, won," he smirks.

Lava fills me and all I see is red hot rage as I stare him down. Everything about him stands out here. From his designer jeans to his red Polo shirt. He screams money and cockiness and judgement.

"Why can't you just stay on your side of town?" I yell again.

I throw off my helmet and the guy's eyes go wide like saucers. For a moment, he is stunned as he realizes he just raced against a girl.

"Oh shit, you are a chick," he says, more to himself than to anyone else. The humor filling his features only intensifies the raging anger brewing deep inside of me.

"Hell yeah, I'm a girl. I should have won that race, but you showed up on your super expensive bike and didn't play fair," I screech.

"Stella, you really need to calm down," Tank says, stepping in front of me.

"Did you hear how she is yelling at him? Doesn't she know who he is?" I hear someone whisper behind me. Fear laces their voice and I take just a second to think that over.

Spinning, I eye the crowd, looking for the source of the words. Why would I give two shits who this guy is? Just because he has money, doesn't mean he is anyone important.

"She's fine. Let her be pissed. I won this race, and I did it fairly. I didn't do anything underhanded," the guy explains.

"You don't understand, I needed to win that race. I needed that money," I shout back at him.

He stares back at me. A blank expression blankets his chiseled face. Why is he so gorgeous? It's almost unfair.

"I don't come from wealth like you do," I snap. "I have bills to pay. I owe people money and that money that you just lost me..." I couldn't even think about what would happen if I didn't find a way to get a thousand dollars. A shiver runs through me, and he watches me with careful precision.

"You don't know a damn thing about me," he snaps back at me.

I don't expect the anger resonating from his voice, and I feel my legs shake under the wrath in his eyes.

"Obviously, she has no clue who he is, or she wouldn't be yelling like that," another person says from the crowd.

Now, I am beyond infuriated and a tad bit curious. Why are people talking about him as though I should know who he is? Is this guy some celebrity?

Turning to the crowd gathered around us, I yell, "Alright, who is he? Why are all of you staring at him like he's someone special and not just some rich prick who decided to slum it tonight?"

A few people snicker until they see the seriousness on my face, and then they quiet back down.

Tank leans in close to me and I smell weed and booze lingering around him. "This is Micah Lee. His father is part of the Antoni Mafia Family. Baby girl, you just started a war with the devil," Tank says into my ear.

A shudder runs through me as his words register in my brain. I had been so lost in my own anger and emotions, that I didn't even bother to find out who he was. Now that I know, I realize that my night just went from bad to worse. The Antoni Mafia Family is Savannah's most notorious crime family. They rule the streets and everyone who they encounter bows down to them. They aren't just a family—they are a kingdom.

A kingdom that rules Savannah with an iron fist and takes no mercy. Yeah, I had heard the rumors and stories about the Antoni Mafia Family, but I never thought I would find myself at the mercy of one of their children. Why was my life so miserable? I swear, I couldn't catch a break.

"So, what if I am part of the Antoni Mafia Family. That doesn't have anything to do with what I'm doing here tonight," Micah says, glaring daggers my way.

I see how everyone adoringly looks at him like he is some god. I can't help but dislike him even more knowing that he isn't just rich, but royalty, too.

"It has everything to do with you being here. Look around, the people that live here don't just race to have fun. This is our livelihood," I say, waving my hands around me.

A few people nod in agreement, but none actually say anything. They are too afraid. I see it in their eyes, and it makes me sick.

"You can keep the money, I don't need it," Micah says, like that makes him some knight in shining armor.

Shaking my head, I refuse to be some charity case for this guy. It doesn't work that way around here. We all earn our money-- it isn't just handed to us like it is in his world. "No way. I may need the money, but I won't take it like this," I say, shoving past him.

He barely moves as I push him. As I make my way back over to my bike, I feel hot tears forming in my eyes, but I won't let them fall here. I won't give Micah the satisfaction of knowing he hurt me. Jumping on my bike, I throw on my helmet and speed away. As I drive back toward the trailer park, I allow my tears and raw emotion to finally consume me.

Somehow, I have to find a way to get that money.

CHAPTER SIX

MICAH

What was her problem?

That fiery blonde sure was out of control as she had that little outburst. The crowd is still staring at me as we watch the taillights of her bike drive away.

"Hey, don't let Stella get to you, Micah," I hear someone say beside me.

Shrugging my shoulders, I turn to Tank, the guy who set up this race. "She doesn't bother me," I say, though I feel a lump beginning to form in my chest.

I have seen girls get angry before. Especially, after I had hooked up with them and then left them once we were finished. They would scream, cry, and stomp their feet like dramatic little toddlers. If anything, it had made me laugh watching their hysterics. But something about the way Stella reacted, had an unsettling feeling growing deep inside of me. There was an emotional storm that erupted from her, one that came from real pain and agony.

Tank goes to hand me the money, but I shake my head, no. "I didn't come here to make any money," I tell him.

Tank's eyes go wide as he looks from the large stash of bills in his hand and then back to me. "Man, this is a lot of money," he says.

I glance around and start to notice how much I truly stand out around here. Everyone is wearing torn or dirty clothes, off brand shoes, and I see the decrepit buildings all around us. This is the 'bad' side of town where poverty is the norm and money like this is hard to come by.

"Yeah," I agree, though in my world, a thousand bucks barely covers a purse for my mom. "Give it to that girl, Stella," I reply.

That wild look in her eyes is now cemented in my eyes. I shudder at the thought, which causes alarm bells to wail all through me. Why do I care so much what that chick thinks? We are from different worlds, but still, I feel guilt creeping over me, and I hate that feeling. Hell, I hate any feelings.

"I doubt she will take it. Stella may need the money, but she has a stubborn streak and is prideful. She drives me crazy, but I respect the hell out of her," Tank admits, chuckling as he thinks of her.

I had only just met Stella, but I saw that pride and stubbornness that Tank was describing. I knew it wasn't any of my business, but I couldn't help but ask, "Why does she need that money so bad? Can't her parents help her out?"

A girl who has long legs, jet black hair, and piercings all along her right ear, struts over to us. Tank smiles as she nestles against him, and I can tell she is his girl. "You may not know us," the girl begins, "but we all know who you are. Stella doesn't have parents to ask for anything. Her mom is MIA, and she never knew her dad. Stella is good people, though, and has to fight for the little amount that she has. Don't get it twisted, rich boy, you don't belong around here," she sneers.

That twist of pain resurfaces, and I hate how it is killing the high from my race. Hearing that Stella is basically on her own, just makes me feel like shit. That crazy look in her eyes wasn't just from her anger from losing to me, but it was from years of being alone. In my world, I never went without anything. My parents loved me and showered me with gifts and more money than I probably needed. I guess sometimes, I forget that there are people out there less fortunate than me. Who have it tough and don't live like royalty.

Tank looks uncomfortable for a moment. He whispers something in her ear, and she scowls, but gives me a menacing look before she turns and walks away. Her words strike me. I had never been made to feel unwanted anywhere. Hell, people around Savannah pay me and the rest of my gang to just show up to their parties. Being part of the Antoni Mafia Family makes me powerful and popular, but for some reason, around here I am the one looked down on. I have never felt this way before...and I don't like it.

"Ignore Rose, she is just..."

I cut him off before he could finish. "No need to explain. Look, I see that me being here is clearly causing a problem. I will just head out," I tell him.

Tank just nods knowing that I'm right. Why I thought coming down to this side of Savannah to race was a good idea, is beyond me. I just wanted a new thrill-- a new place to get wild, but what I got was an uneasy feeling. Tank gives me the money, even though I refused it. I stuff it in my back pocket and get the hell out of that place.

***

The next day, I'm lounging out by the pool when Gabby plops down beside me on one of the sun chairs.

Her red hair is pinned up in a tight bun and her green eyes sparkle against the bright afternoon sun. It's Sunday, and we like to relax on this day.

"What's wrong with you?" Gabby asks, as she places large, black sunglasses over her eyes.

"Nothing," I mumble out.

Closing my eyes, I try and pretend like I had fallen asleep, but Gabby knows better.

"Don't pull that with me, Micah. You aren't hung over because you didn't go out partying last night. Ason and Talon are playing video games in Ason's theatre room, and they didn't mention anything about you all fighting, so something else is going on," she states matter-of-factly.

I hate how Gabby always knows when something is wrong with the guys. She may not be my blood, but she's my sister and my family. I know she won't stop pestering me unless I explain what happened, so I just sigh and open my mouth. "I had a race last night that didn't go as planned," I begin.

I hear Gabby laugh. "Did you finally lose?" she asks, enjoying that thought way too much.

"No, I didn't lose," I grumble out. "I won..."

I let that linger in the air for a moment. I hear the chair shift as Gabby sits up. Even though my eyes are closed, I can feel her watching me.

"So, what's the problem then?" she questions.

I know that I might as well continue. I'm not in the mood for Gabby to ask me a million questions. "I went down to the warehouse district and raced a track there," I began, sitting up and slowly opening my eyes. "When I won, this chick named, Stella, lost her temper and started screaming at me."

"Micah, isn't that the normal for you? I mean, you tend to upset the ladies when you love them and eave them," she scoffs.

I hang my head low and stare at the concrete beneath my bare feet. The sun is blazing on my skin and I feel like I'm on fire now. "This was different. She was mad because of the money, not the title of winner. Apparently, she needed the money really bad," I say.

That strange feeling in the pit of my stomach returns and I desperately feel the need to go grab some alcohol or weed. I hate this and want nothing more than to numb any of that away.

"Your first mistake was going down to that part of Savannah. Around here, people care about status and money. In the poverty-stricken areas of Savannah, it's all about survival. I've dealt with a few guys from that area, and I know how different it may seem. Almost like you've traveled to another world. Money doesn't come easy for everyone and what you did was take away her means for survival," Gabby explains.

If I didn't feel like shit before, I certainly do now. I've never been ashamed of anything in my life. But right now, for some strange reason, I feel ashamed of coming from a good home and life. I don't have to fight for what I have. The battle for the kingdom I so much enjoy was fought for me by my father and the other members of the Antoni Mafia Family.

"Damn, this is really messed up," I sigh.

"Well, what are you going to do about it?" she asks me.

"Nothing," I say, shrugging my shoulders. "What can I do?"

"Give her the money. That girl obviously needs it more than you do," Gabby insists.

She's right; but I have no idea how to give the money to Stella. I don't know anything about her other than she hates me and has a fiery temper. And... she's hot as hell. I had never seen someone as beautiful as she was. Even when she was screaming at me, I couldn't help but notice her plump, perfect lips and the way her jeans hugged her thin waist. Shaking my head, I try to fight my body from reacting to her. We came from different worlds and besides, she clearly hated everything that I represented. Not that I could blame her now that I think about it.

"I don't know where she lives," I try and argue.

Gabby stands and throws her pink sequin cover up over her body. "How did you find out about the race in the first place?" she asked, placing a hand on her hip.

"A guy at one of my races gave me the number of Tank. He's in charge of organizing the races and taking bets," I tell her.

"Ok, contact him. Man, Micah. For someone with such good grades, you are pretty dumb. Use your head. Reach out to that Tank guy. Get her address and then return the money."

I let Gabby's insult slide for now. As much as I hate to relive any of the events from last night, I know that this is the right thing to do. Even if Stella wouldn't take the money from me, maybe I could leave it in her mailbox or something once I got her address. If I made this right, maybe this shitty feeling would go away.

"Fine, I'll text him now," I say, grabbing my phone that was lying on top of my pool towel.

I type out the text quickly and then fall back in the chair again. Gabby begins to stomp away, and I have no doubt that she's going to find Ason and Talon and share my situation with them. She pauses right before she walks inside the back door of the house. Turning, she gives me a serious look.

"Micah, whatever happens, don't let this girl or anyone stop you from doing what's right for our family. You have to start thinking about your future and the casino," she tells me, then stomps inside, allowing the thick, heavy door to slam behind her.

Shaking my head, I throw myself back onto the lounge chair. I refuse to allow some chick to get into my head like this. Regardless of what anyone says, I am going to get rid of this money, Stella, and any sense of caring for her that I feel. I have a future to think about and it doesn't involve Stella.

Chapter Seven

Stella

A pounding in my head wakes me way too fucking early.

No. That pounding isn't in my head, it's coming from the front door. Throwing my covers off my body, I roll out of bed and pad through the trailer until I reach the front door. I'm too tired to think clearly, so I just pull the door open without taking a second to glance out the window to see who is bothering me at such an early hour.

I wish I had thought this through.

Standing on my porch is Lucas, sweat already beading on his greasy forehead. An angry scowl greets me, and I let out a heavy breath at the sight of his frumpy frame.

"What do you want, Lucas?" I ask, holding up my hand to block the blinding sunlight from my eyes.

Damn, it's already hot out and I can already tell that the humidity is going to be brutal today. Lucas sneers as he wipes a trail of sweat from his face.

"Fuck, Stella. I want my damn money," he spits out.

The money.

Fuck. My. Life.

I had been so angry when I got home last night, that I had downed a bottle of tequila that I found in the kitchen cabinets, leftover from one of my mom's parties. She may not leave me groceries or money to pay bills, but I can always count on her to leave booze.

"Lucas..." I begin stumbling over my own words, knowing that I'm pissing him off even more.

Stomping his foot, I feel the vibration of the movement under my feet. Lucas yells at me, spittle flying out of his mouth. "You fucking bitch," he roars out. "I told you that I wasn't going to wait any longer. Give me my money or I will make you pay me in other ways," he says, reaching out and running his finger along my bare arm.

I am instantly aware that I am standing before him in only a pair of short sleeping shorts and a tank top. My skin crawls under his touch and I want to vomit from the images his words evoke in me.

"I have it," I lie.

My mind is racing as I struggle to find something more to say. Lucas calms down a little, but his eyes raise as he glances at me with a suspicious stare. He isn't as dumb as I wish he were, and that terrifies me more than anything else.

"Then where is it?" he asks, his eyes raking over my body.

Crossing my arms over my chest, I do my best to shield his eyes from my body, but it's no use. Why is this my life? Why can't I be one of those people who has parents they can rely on and who doesn't have to worry about pervy landlords.

"It's in my kitchen. Hold on and I will go get the money," I say, trying to stall him.

I have to put a barrier between me and Lucas for now-- at least until I can figure something out. Before Lucas can react, I reach out and slam the door in his face, locking the deadbolt. Lucas begins pounding on the door and wiggling the handle. This place is barely holding on and for a second, I fear he may break the door down. Thankfully, luck holds out on me as the door holds up. I know it won't last long, so I rush to my room and put on a pair of Nike shoes that I bought from Goodwill, and then run out the back door. As I run toward my bike, I can hear Lucas cursing at me as he continues to pound against the front door.

My bike is sitting under the tarp I use to shield it from the weather and neighbors with sticky fingers. Throwing off the tarp, I jump on the bike and put it in neutral so that I can get a good start before I have to turn the ignition. I manage to get a few trailers away before I am able to start my bike and drive off.

For a brief moment, I feel a sense of relief as I drive away. Though, just like everything else in my life, I know this reprieve is only temporary as life will eventually come crashing back down on me again.

***

Hours later, I make my way back to my trailer.

After I had escaped Lucas, I drove through Savannah and then hung out down by the river walk for a while. I needed to clear my head and find a peaceful place to allow my racing nerves to calm down. Now, as I make my way back home, that terrible feeling of unease creeps back over me. For most people, home is a sanctuary-- a place where you go for love, comfort, and safety. Unfortunately for me, home doesn't hold those same feelings for me. No. For me, home is unsteady, unwelcoming, and unsafe. One day, I will escape the hell hole that I am forced to live in right now. But that day sure as hell can't some soon enough.

Pulling into the small gravel parking space next to my trailer, I notice that the front door is wide open and broken shards of wood lay scattered all over the rotting porch. Sighing, I know that I will also need to find some money to pay to have that repaired. Lucas sure as hell won't be fixing it.

Parking my bike, I throw the tarp back over it and then head over to the front door to closely inspect the damage. I will more than likely need to call Ally and see if I can sleep at her place tonight. It won't be safe for me to stay here tonight with a broken front door. There are too many bad men around here who would love nothing more than to find me vulnerable and unable to hide from them.

The wooden steps creak under my feet as I move to the door. The door handle is lying on the floor inside the trailer and the front door is bended in, from where Lucas obviously kicked it in.

"Damn," I mutter to myself.

As I stand there, frozen and unable to think clearly, I hear a car pull up in front of my trailer. Great, is it Lucas to finally make me pay, or is it one of the drug dealers or pimps who constantly hound me to work for them. Either way, I'm fucked.

As I spin around, ready to yell and scream at whoever dared to stop, my body goes rigid as I spot the last person I ever expected to see again.

Micah

Wearing a pair of dark denim jeans that hang dangerously low on his hips, Micah runs a hand through his sandy blonde hair. He opens the rusted mailbox with my trailer number written in Sharpie, and stares back at me.

Micah.

What the hell is he doing here? How the hell does he know where I live? And, more importantly, why is he placing a large envelope in my mailbox?

CHAPTER EIGHT

MICAH

I've never been in such a run-down, sad part of town before.

When I ventured to the warehouse district, I thought that was the worst part of Savannah. However, this was far worse. Driving through the trailer park, I couldn't help but stare at the broken-down trailers that were in desperate need of repairs and new paint. Women in barely any clothing walked through the uneven street, eyes glazed over, and waving and calling at me. Kids ran around barefoot and dirty, no adults in sight to watch out for them. Then, there was Stella's trailer.

I knew that when I made a decision to come down here, I would be driving into a different world. Still, I never expected to find such depravity. I pulled my white Range Rover over and prayed the gravel wouldn't scratch the paint of my freshly waxed car. With the envelope filed with the money tightly in my hands, I got out of my car and walked over to the mailbox which looked like it would fall over with just a simple touch. The air was thick and humid, but a stench of weed and garbage filtered through the air and my stomach churn. This was like some third-world country.

A woman smoking on her porch watched me with curious eyes. Her hair was in disarray and her clothes hung off her too thin frame. Trying not to make eye contact with her, I picked up the pace as I moved toward the mailbox. However, something caught my attention from the trailer. The door was wide open and bent. Clearly, someone had broken in. A strange sense of urgency rushed through me as I thought about Stella living here.

She was beautiful beyond the normal standards of beauty. Sure, she had a rough exterior clearly created from living in such a dangerous world, but she also had soft eyes and a body that made my dick stand at attention every time I thought about her. When she straddled her bike, my mind imagined it was my cock that she was riding instead. When those perky lips were yelling at me, I imagined them wrapped around my dick. She was sexy as hell and had no business living in a place like this.

Movement causes my heart to stir and then I spot Stella moving to the doorway. Frozen in place, I watch as her face falls and that determined, strong look that was evident on face the night we met, is gone now. She looks scared and unsure. For some reason, this makes me feel a pain in my heart. Stella should never look so sad.

Letting out an exasperated sigh, she turns and locks eyes with me.

Fuck, I'm caught now.

Her eyes grow wide like saucers and her lips turn down in a frown. That feisty side of her that turned me on is back, but now, I am fearful for what she is about to do.

"What the fuck are you doing here?" she roars out, storming out of the trailer.

She closes the distance between us in record speed and I have no idea what to do.

"Hello to you, too," I say, smiling back at her.

I can feel the heat from her wrath as she glares daggers at me. She's not amused by my presence or attempt to be cordial. Hell, we both know that I was being a little cocky, anyway. I quickly realize that messing with this girl is fun—a turn on even. She's fucking hot when she's pissed.

"Cut the bullshit. Why are you here? I really don't have time to deal with your rich boy antics," she states coldly.

I take a moment and really focus on her features. Her cheeks are red and stained from tears. She looks exhausted and I want to ask her what is wrong, but I doubt she would tell me anyway. Holding up the envelope, I know that I'm making a risky move, but I need to do what I came here to do and get the hell out of this place before someone tries to kill me. And, I believe that *someone* would be Stella.

"Look, I didn't come here to cause any trouble. I just wanted to bring you the earnings. I don't need it and I think you could use it..." I begin, but am quickly cut off.

Throwing her arms up in the air wildly, Stella lets out a shriek. "I am not some charity case. I don't want or need anything from you," she yells, shoving me with her tiny hands.

I don't move an inch from her attempt to shove me. In fact, I let out a slight chuckle which only infuriates Stella more.

"Do you think this is funny? Coming down to the trailer park to bring money to the poor girl? Does it make you feel like you have done your good deed for the year? I don't care who you are or how dangerous the mafia that you belong to is. This isn't a game. This is my life and I need you to leave me the hell alone," she cries out.

Stella's body begins to tremble, and I see her trying to wipe tears away from her eyes. I can tell that for Stella, showing any sign of weakness is dangerous. Living here, she has to be strong. Knowing that she doesn't have a family only makes me feel a stronger desire to help her. As much as her outburst frustrates me, it's also hot as hell and creates a fire inside of me. Stella has no one to look out for her, and for some reason that I can't explain, I want to be the person who she can rely on.

To protect her.

To save her.

She's still cursing when I reach out and grab her around her tiny waist, pulling her toward me. Stella's eyes go wide, but I don't give her an opportunity to fight me or yell at me again. Crashing my lips on hers, I stop her from talking and allow my kiss to quiet down the raging storm brewing inside of her. As our kiss deepens, I feel her body relax as she allows herself to give in to me.

My tongue slips between her lips and she gladly accepts it, opening her mouth a little more. My hands grip her hips tightly and her hands move to my hair. Her fingers massage my head, and it feels incredible. After a few moments, Stella pulls away and we are both panting as we attempt to catch our breath.

"What was...Why did you..." Stella can't form a complete sentence and I think it's cute as hell.

"You needed to stop yelling and relax," I answer, even though she didn't actually ask me a question.

Her body had called out to me. She needed something to calm her raging nerves and thankfully, that was my kiss.

She stares back at me with her hands on her hips. I take in her body and notice that she's wearing a pair of shorts that barely cover her ass and the tank top shows cleavage from her ample breasts. Damn, Stella is sexy as hell, and I don't think she sees it in herself.

"I didn't ask you to help me," she says quietly.

It's the first time I've seen her calm and I revel in the moment. I can't imagine how it must feel to always be on edge. To not have a moment of peace in your life.

"I know that you didn't ask me, but I wanted to do this. I'm not pitying your or trying to treat you like some charity case. You were right at the race; I had no business being in that race. I don't need the money and if I hadn't had been there, you would have won, hands down."

Stella just looks at me and I can tell she is trying to figure out what to say. I've obviously thrown her off being kind.

"I need the money, but not like this..." she goes to argue.

"Just take it. It looks to me like you have some repairs to make," I say, pointing behind her to the broken door of her trailer.

Stella sighs and doesn't bother to look behind her. "Yeah, and for rent, food, and everything else," she whispers.

I'm not sure if I was meant to hear that, but it rocks me to my core. "Were you racing to pay for rent and food?" I ask.

All Stella does is nod. She looks embarrassed and her eyes focus on her feet. I don't want her to feel like this. No one who works that hard to take care of herself should ever feel embarrassed.

I take my hand and place it under her chin, forcing her to look up at me. "Stella, you are beautiful, strong, and resilient. Don't be embarrassed over circumstances that you can't control. Just take this money and let me help you," I offer again.

There's a softness radiating from Stella right now, and I want to be the person who brings that light back into her eyes. Life is so unfair. I was born into wealth and power. I never did anything to deserve this life, but it's mine. Same for Stella. She didn't ask to be born into a world where she had to survive on her own.

"I won't be able to repay you," Stella states.

"I don't want you to," I respond.

Shaking her head, Stella steps back and out of my touch. "There has to be something," she says, biting her lip in angst.

Damn, it's hot as hell when she does that.

"Maybe you can show me some racing tricks," I offer.

The reality is, I don't need help with racing. Anything I needed to learn; I paid a few pro racers to help me with when I first started this hobby. But, if it makes Stella feel more comfortable taking my money, I'll do it.

"Ok, I can do that," she agrees. I slide the envelope into her hand and this time, she accepts the offer. Holding it closely to her side, she smiles, and it appears genuine. "Thank you."

"You don't have to thank me," I tell her. I go to move, but then I am reminded of the broken door. "Hey, what are you going to do about that door? You can't stay here tonight," I deadpan.

"I have a friend I can stay with tonight," Stella offers. "Thanks for asking though," she says, seeming to fidget with the hem of her shorts. I can tell she is uncomfortable with this.

"No problem. I will be in touch," I say.

Stella pauses and glances back at me. "Hey, do you want something to drink?" she asks.

I doubt this girl has anything that I would want, but the fact that she's offering surely means something.

"Sure," I reply, following her inside the trailer.

The place is outdated, but Stella has kept it clean. An old, brown couch sits against a white wall and only a coffee table fills the rest of the space. The kitchen area is smaller than my closet at home, but the counters are bare and wiped down. I can't help but look around and I feel Stella watching me with curious eyes. I know that she's waiting for me to judge her—but she's got it all wrong.

Stella can't be faulted for the life she was thrown into. Her surroundings aren't her own doing and I actually respect her for surviving in spite of the shitty cards she was dealt in life.

I spot a book lying on the coffee table and I pick it up, inspecting the worn cover.

"A Streetcar Named Desire," I say aloud.

Reaching out, Stella grabs the book from me and places it back on the coffee table. "It's just something my mom gave me once," she says, shaking her head like it's insignificant.

She hands me a bottle of water and I gladly accept the gift.

"What is it?" I ask her, clearly amused by her shyness.

A tight line forms over her lips. "When my mom found out she was pregnant with me, she was seventeen and still in high school. Her class was reading this novel and she loved the character, Stella. I guess it stuck and that's where my name came from. A few years ago, I found the book in the back of her closet. She gave it to me and told me it's significance. It's stupid really," she chuckles lightly, looking away from me.

Grabbing her hand, I force Stella to look at me. "It's not stupid. If it means something to you, then it's important," I state flatly.

When Stella's eyes reach mine, there's a spark that causes my heart to leap into my throat. I can't deny my attraction to this girl, but there's something else that draws me to her like a magnet, but I can't explain it.

"Well, I need to go," I tell her.

"Ok. Thanks for today," Stella says.

I don't trust myself to stay here alone with Stella any longer. Every part of me is screaming to kiss her and claim her as my own. I know that it's wrong, so I turn to leave.

"Bye, Stella," I yell, as I begin walking toward my Range Rover.

Stella remains standing as she watches me leave. My dick is throbbing right now, and I knew that if I didn't get out of there soon, I wouldn't be able to control myself any longer. Stella does something to me that I just can't explain. There this sexual friction created when I am near her. It both terrifies and excites me.

I have no idea what I'm going to do about Stella, but I am eager to find out.

Chapter Nine

Stella

The taste of Micah lingered on my lips well into the evening.

Peppermint and a hint of smoke are now my favorite tastes and I hate myself for giving in to him like that.

When I had found Micah outside my house, there was a range of emotions that had taken over me.

Anger.

Shock.

Embarrassment.

The cocky, asshole who I had met the other night at the race wasn't the guy who had shown up at my home. Micah was a different person today. He showed me a kindness that I hadn't seen before. I expected him to laugh at me and berate me as the poor, white trash girl who he was throwing money at. Instead, Micah calmed my nerves and the brewing storm that never seemed to settle inside of me.

And, he had kissed me with so much passion, I thought my body will melt under his touch.

Now, sitting on my front porch, I watch as the sunset starts to fade over the horizon. Oranges, reds, and purples dance across the sky and I can't help but wonder if the sunsets over on Micah's side of town look the same. Do people with money even take time to admire the way the sky glows like magic when the world shifts from day to night? They probably have too many beautiful things in their lives to care about something nature provides.

"Look who decided to show her face again," a snarky voice says.

All of the beauty and majesty that I was once admiring seems to fade away as Lucas makes his way toward me. I knew that once he heard I was back, it wouldn't be too long before he came back to get what he wanted.

An arrogant grin is plastered over his face and his beer belly jiggles as he struts toward me. He thinks I don't have the money. He thinks he will get to have his filthy way with me.

"I just had to get the money," I tell him, standing up.

This time, I changed into a more modest t-shirt and a pair of jeans. Now, standing before him, I feel confident as I know I hold the power now.

Lucas laughs at me, and I can see that he thinks he's got me where he wants me. "Stella, let's stop playing games right now. We both know that you don't have the money. How about we go inside and find a way to work something out," he says, licking his lips.

I feel vomit rising in my throat, but I manage to reign in my anger. "No, that's not necessary." I pull out the thousand dollars Micah had given me and hand it over to Lucas. "This covers last month's rent and this month's rent. Plus, to get the front door repaired," I tell him.

Lucas looks taken aback as he takes the money from me. He counts it twice before looking back at me.

"How did you get this? That whore mother of yours hasn't been back yet," Lucas sneers.

I flinch at his insult, but I don't let him get to me. "Don't worry about how I got the money, just take it," I snap.

Lucas takes a step toward me, and I hate how close he is to me. I hold my ground and make sure he doesn't know that I'm really trembling inside.

"Well, since you made me wait for so long, I had to add a little tax to the amount owed," Lucas says.

Fuck, no. I don't know why I thought this would be easy. Nothing is ever easy for me. Lucas can't just accept the money and leave me alone. He has to continue to destroy my already shitty life. He also knows that there is no one to call or get to help me. The police barely make their way down this way anymore. The only sirens we hear are the ones from paramedics or the coroner. There's no one to rescue me now.

"Lucas, you got your money. Just leave me alone now," I plead with him.

The sunlight is gone now and the broken streetlights barely provide enough light for me to see anything around me. Still, I can see the anger glowing from Lucas and it pains me that he can't just allow me to have one free moment.

"You are awful brave right now, Stella. If I don't leave you alone, what are you going to do?" he asks, his face now mere inches from mine. "We both know that you don't have anyone to call. There's no one to save you," he seethes.

His hot, steady breaths are making my stomach churn and I have to hold my fists at my sides, so I don't haul off and punch him in the face.

"Get the fuck away from her," I hear, roaring from the street.

Lucas spins around and when we both spot Micah and his Range Rover, I swear, we both let out a gasp.

Micah rushes up to us and shoves Lucas aside. Lucas stumbles, but catches himself on the railing along the steps. He releases a string of curses as he rights himself again.

"Who the hell are you?" Lucas spits at Micah.

I back away from them, unsure of what is about to happen. "I'm your worst nightmare if you ever touch her again," Micah whispers, the harsh tone sending cold shills down my spine.

Lucas looks between me and Micah and from his startled expression, I can tell that he is confused right now. Rich guys like Micah don't venture out to the trailer park unless they are buying drugs or looking for hookers.

"Is this your pimp?" Lucas asks, and I feel like I've been slapped across the face.

Though, before I can respond, Micah leans in and talks to Lucas. His voice is low, but I can still hear what he's saying. "My father is part of the Antoni Mafia Family. I don't think they would like it if I told them some old man was bullying a high school girl."

Lucas's eyes bulge and he visibly shakes now. We all know the meaning behind Micah's words. The Antoni Mafia can make people disappear and I doubt very many people would miss Lucas. The kiss Micah and I had shared had rocked my world, but watching him stand up for me, is doing something else to my heart, body, and soul. No one has ever rescued me. No one has ever cared enough to defend me. And now, this rich boy who is part of the mafia has come to do all of those things. I feel like I'm living in a dream because nothing good ever happens to me.

Lucas finally nods and then walks away. I'm left standing there with Micah, my body shaking, and my eyes glued to the beautiful boy before me. He looks so out of place right now, like a diamond thrown in a pile of garbage.

"Come on, you need to get out of here," Micah says, reaching out to take my hand.

"Wait, what?" I ask, flabbergasted. I take a step back, so he can't touch me. To be honest, I'm afraid that if he were to touch me, I wouldn't be able to say no. "Why did you come back?" I yell out.

"My guys have an informant around here and they told me that Lucas was heading toward your trailer. I turned around and came back. I'm going to take you some place where you can be safe. Do you have any family or friends nearby?" he asks, as he turns to head toward his SUV. Micah doesn't stop walking until he opens the driver's side door to his Range

Rover. When he realizes that I'm not behind him, he pauses. "What are you doing?"

Shaking my head, I finally find my voice again. "I don't have any family to go to." I'm humiliated by my circumstances right now. "My friend, Ally, lives close. I can go stay with her," I finally say.

There are no words to truly express how I feel about what Micah has told me. He has informants watching Lucas? He just decided to come back and what? Save me? I never knew guys like this existed until I met Micah.

"Ok, I will take you to her house," he says, jumping into the driver's seat and closing the door.

I wait a moment and then slowly walk up to the car. When I open the door, the scent of leather billows out of the interior and I can't help but inhale the sweet scent. I've never smelled it before, and I can see why people love it so much. As I sit down, my body conforms to the seat. My eyes dance around the interior and admire the wood and chrome design. I've never been in anything this fancy and clean and I almost feel like just being here dirties the space. Seeing my trepidation, Micah chances a glance my way.

"What's wrong?" he asks, as he starts the engine.

"I feel very out of place in this car," I say honestly. Especially, after he was just inside the trash can I call a home.

"Why?" Micah asks me. He looks so handsome with the slight glow of the interior lights. His chiseled jaw makes him look like a Greek God.

I can't help but laugh at this. "I don't exactly look like someone who should be sitting in an expensive car."

Micah pulls away from my trailer and I can see his jaw tense. I get the vibe that he wants to say something, but he allows silence to take over for a few minutes. Finally, he speaks. "I think you look great sitting my car."

His words strike me, and I am thankful that it's dark inside. My cheeks burn from the heat rising to my face. Micah does something to me and I hate how my body reacts to him. We come from two different worlds and would never work out, but still, I can't help but enjoy the feelings he evokes in me.

"Why did you show up here tonight?" I ask. The question had been in the back of my mind since I first saw him, but everything happened so fast, I didn't get a chance to ask until now.

Micah looks at me and I see a look of anger flash through his eyes. "I was worried about your front door. I didn't like the idea of you staying here tonight without a way to shut out the world." He shakes his head, and chuckles a little. "I am not handy or anything and honestly, I'm not really sure what I expected to do, but I just needed to check on you."

The fact that he cared enough to check on me doesn't go unnoticed. I don't know how to respond to that. I feel uncomfortable accepting any help from people. I'm so used to figuring things out on my own, but I am grateful that he decided to come anyway.

"That wasn't necessary, but I appreciate it," I say quietly.

"So, where exactly am I taking you?" he asks, as he pulls out onto the main road. He's clearly just as uncomfortable as I am right now.

"Turn right at the stop sign," I begin, providing him with directions to Ally's.

I take out my phone and type a quick text to her.

Me: On my way to your place. Can't stay at the trailer.

Ally replies instantly and I wonder what she will think when I arrive in a Range Rover.

Ally: Ok, I will be waiting.

When we finally pull up outside of Ally's trailer, Micah stops, but doesn't turn off the engine.

Ally appears at the doorway and when she sees us, her eyes go wide, and a devious smile appears on her face. Rolling my eyes, I quickly open the door of the car.

"Hey, let me have your number," Micah says, snagging my phone out of my hand.

I didn't expect him to ask, nor to steal my phone. Ally comes toward us, and I hear her whistle.

"Wow, nice car!" she admires.

I turn and glare at her, mouthing for her to shut up. Ally only laughs though. When Micah is finished, he hands me back my phone.

"Thanks for the ride," I say, and then close the door.

Micah smiles and then drives away. Ally and I stand side-by-side as we watch his taillights fade away. Once the Range Rover is out of sight, Ally smacks me in the arm.

"I believe you have a LOT to tell me," she says, grabbing my hand and leading me toward her trailer.

We walk inside and head straight for her bedroom. Unlike my trailer, Ally's is clean and feels warm and inviting. She and her mom may not have a lot, but they keep a nice home and I always like staying here. Sadly, Ally's mom works a lot, so she isn't home right now. She works late shifts at a small diner and I commend her for doing everything she can to take care of Ally.

Ally flops down on her twin bed and eyes me. "Alright, spill it."

I lay down beside her. There isn't a lot of room, but it's still comfortable. "There really isn't much to tell. Lucas was being a dick, as usual, and even after I gave him the money for rent, he wanted more. Micah just showed up and surprised both of us," I said.

"Wow, I think he likes you," Ally giggles.

"No way. If anything, he feels bad for me. He's rich and can have any girl he wants. I doubt the girl from the trailer park is his type," I say, and the words sting me.

"Stella, the way he was looking at you tonight, that isn't pity—that was lust. Besides, a guy just doesn't show up to save a girl that he doesn't have feelings for," Ally says, turning to face me.

I pull the faded My Little Pony bedspread up to cover my body. Ally has had this thing since we were five-years-old. It was a gift from Santa, and I remembered being so jealous that Santa brought her presents. I always thought that I was bad, and that's why I didn't get anything. Now, I know it's because my mom was probably passed out or didn't have money for presents because she blew it on drugs and booze. This blanket reminds me of a time before I knew the horrors of the world. Before I was drawn into anger and had to choose survival over happiness.

"Either way, it doesn't matter. We come from different worlds, so it would never work," I say, rolling over and closing my eyes.

Thankfully, Ally takes the hint and grows quiet. I hear her scrolling through TikTok, but she doesn't say anything else. As I fall into a deep slumber, I can't get Micah's face out of my mind.

Chapter Ten

Micah

"Dude, you just shot me," Talon yells out.

Shaking my head, I focus my eyes back on the television screen and notice that I just took out Talon's character in our video game.

"Shit. Sorry, dude," I say, throwing my controller next to me on the sofa.

Talon shakes his head at me. "We are on the same team. We were winning," he shouts, throwing his controller across the room.

I watch as it slams against the wall and breaks into a million little pieces. It's nothing around here for us to be screaming and cursing at one another.

"Where is your head at, Micah?" Talon asks me.

Rubbing my eyes, I don't even try to mask my emotions right now. The guys can already tell when something is up with me, and Talon is relentless. He would push me until I told him anyway.

"Remember when I told you about that crazy chick from the race the other night," I begin.

Talon raises his eyes at me. "Don't tell me you fucked her and now she's going all stalker on you," he states wildly.

Men in the mafia always sleep around-- at least until they are married. Most Capo's have a goomah; a mistress or two on the side, but not the Antoni Mafia Family men. We believe in settling down with only one woman once we get married. So, for most men in the mafia, having a few crazy bitches that linger around is normal.

Gabby steps into the room, her Louis Vuitton shoes slapping against the hardwood floor. She rolls her eyes at us like we are nothing but mere children.

"So, what did I miss?" Gabby asks, plopping down next to me on the sofa. She is wearing a skin-tight black dress and blood red lipstick. She looks like she's about to go party and not ready for a Sunday dinner with the family. We all stare back at her and she just raises her eyes in confusion. "What?"

"Well, we were sort of having a conversation," I say, looking between Talon and Gabby.

"Oh, please," Gabby says, waving my words away. "I heard enough to know that you have some crazy girl after you," she states with a sneer.

Grunting, I run a hand through my hair in agitation. "That's not what I was saying. I was about to tell Talon that the girl, Stella, got into some trouble and I helped her out. But..." the words hang heavy in the air as I struggle how to finish my sentence.

Gabby stares at me, refusing to look away as she attempts to read me. Talon waits, an unsure look on his serious face.

"What kind of trouble?" Talon finally asks.

Talon has very little patience for my antics, and I know he's trying to figure out if he needs to intervene or not.

"She doesn't have anyone to help her. She doesn't have parents or any family. She pays the rent on some piece of shit trailer just to have a place to live. Her landlord is this pervert who is taking advantage of her and making her pay more money on her rent. I feel like I need to help her out," I finally admit.

Gabby falls back against the leather sofa cushion and Talon whistles as he slaps his hands together.

"I never thought I'd see the day that Micah grows up and realizes that the world doesn't solely revolve around him," Talon bristles.

"Shut up," I growl out.

I know he's messing with me, but at the same time, he's right. I've never cared about other people outside of my circle of friends and family. However, when it comes to Stella, I have this insane, animalistic need—no desire-- to protect her. I know that no one will understand it, but I have to help her, if only to ensure she's safe.

"So, what are you going to do?" Gabby asks.

Unlike Talon, Gabby seems genuinely interested in this strange situation that I have found myself in. Gabby tends to keep to herself and out of all of us, she's the most secretive and holds her own secrets close.

Shaking my head, I sigh. "I don't really know yet, but I will figure it out," I say.

"Everyone needs to meet in the dining room," I hear yelled up to us.

Chance, Talon's dad yells up the stairs to us. We always have Sunday dinner together and then after, the men and women of the mafia meet behind closed doors. It's tradition and in the mafia, you never break tradition.

***

After devouring a delicious Italian feast composed of three types of pastas, two different salads, garlic bread, and enough wine to get half the city of Savannah drunk, we settled in for our weekly meeting. Normally, I just sit back and allow everyone else to make the plans and call the shots. I know my place right now; I'm not a made man and won't be until I prove myself to the family. Still, we have certain jobs we must do to help our fathers. Conversation flows heavily around me, and it isn't until I hear my name being called, that I realize that I haven't been listening at all.

"Micah, what do you say?" my dad asks me.

I glance around the table, and everyone is staring back at me. Aiden, Solly, Gia, Chance, my dad, Talon, and Gabby look at me with narrowed eyes.

"Sorry, what?" I ask, shaking the daze out of my head.

"Micah's been a little focused on a girl," Gabby snickers.

Glaring toward her, my father snaps his fingers at me. "Micah, don't let a girl distract you right now. I asked you if you had given any more though to what you want to do in terms of the casino?" he asks, but now I see anger flaring in his eyes.

I can't disappoint or embarrass my father, especially in front of the rest of the mafia family.

"I think I want to handle some of the new business dealings at the casino," I begin. "There are so many new clubs and restaurants opening in the casino and hotel, I would like to assist with the crews and associates that want to run their businesses through ours," I state.

This is something I can do. I live mostly in the penthouse of the hotel that my parents own in the casino. While I'm only a soldier in our outfit right now, I have the capability to be a Capo one day, just like my father. Though, that day is far away, I still have to pay my dues and show respect to the family.

The men glance around nodding in approval at my words. I felt a weight lift from my chest as I noticed the sign of approval on their serious faces.

"I think that is a good first step," Aiden says. "Though, I think your father and I had other plans for you," he states.

I know what he is referring to. My dad is one of the best snipers around. He earned his way into the Antoni Mafia Family by using his skills. Those are skills he has taught me throughout the years. While I don't always prefer using guns, I can shoot and have one hell of an aim and shot.

Having Aiden's approval is everything, so I know my father is content with this for now. The meeting continues as discussions flare up about potential threats in our arsenal control with a rival mafia family and then the focus turns to profits in our shared business. I nod my head when needed, but my mind is anywhere but here. All I can think about is golden blonde hair, forest green eyes, and a ruthless smile that has stolen my attention.

Chapter Eleven

Stella

The yellow florescent lights hang above me, threatening to suck the life right out of me.

For a Monday, this has to be one of the worst Mondays ever! Ok, maybe I am being a little dramatic, but still. This place feels more like a prison than a school. The cinderblock walls are in desperate need of new paint and the desks have been passed down the last twenty years. Our teachers are exhausted and burned out from dealing with misbehaviors and low pay. My teacher, Mrs. Smith, blabbers in front of the room about the Roman Empire, but no one is even listening. Sadly, this is the only advanced class options, and even in this room, the kids are terrible. I sit in the front of the room, desperately trying to drown out the sounds around me. Unlike my peers, I care about my future. Most people around here stopped believing in happily ever after's once we entered middle school. The reality of the cruel world we were born into did them wrong too many times, and now, they are lost souls. Most will continue in their parents' footsteps; working mindless jobs for minimal pay or will result to working the streets.

A paper wad soars above my head and lands next to Mrs. Smith's feet. She doesn't even blink or stop her lecture. Rumor is, she is retiring next year and drinks heavily on her planning periods, so nothing these kids can do will bother her now. The events from the weekend plagued me all night and I woke up on this Monday feeling more stressed than ever.

Sighing, I focus on her words and my assignment. However, my mind begins to drift away to a gorgeous boy who I have no business thinking about. Micah is rich, popular, and dangerously good looking. Sure, he's helping me out, but it's only because he feels bad for me, and we both know it. He has this need to do a good deed, possibly to fix a wrong he's made in his past.

"Stella, are you ok?" I hear whispered behind me.

Ally pokes my shoulder, knocking me out of my daze. Turning in my seat, I see that she's on her phone, and completely oblivious to the class that is taking place in the front of the room.

"Yeah, why?" I ask.

Ally looks up from her phone, rolling her eyes. "You have been pretty out of it today. When I asked you about the weekend, you blew me off. Something is going on," she persists.

I had told Ally about Micah, since she had seen him drop me off at her place. I acted as though he didn't have any effect on me, but I was only lying to myself. Micha was taking up way too much of my thoughts and I couldn't get lost in a boy that I could never have.

"I guess I am just still shaken up by Lucas," I tell her.

Ally seems content with this response. It's no secret that Lucas has been making my life a living hell ever since I hit puberty and my mom started disappearing for weeks or months at a time. My phone buzzes in my pocket and when I pull it out, I am startled to see Micha's name on my screen.

Micah: What are you doing?

Me: Sitting in class. Shouldn't you be doing the same?

I chuckled lightly to myself as I read his text. I couldn't help but wonder what Micah's school was like. I was sure that he must attend some fancy private school where the kids wear uniforms have butlers and shit like that.

Micah: I'm at lunch. What are you doing this upcoming weekend?

I read his words over a dozen times before I could finally process them. Why did he want to know my plans? This couldn't go too far. Sure, I had let him help me. Once. But that was enough. This couldn't become a 'thing.'

Me: Not sure.

I wrote the vague response and hoped he would get the hint. Don't get me wrong; Micah is everything that a girl could ever dream of in a guy. He has a swagger to him that makes him irresistible and with his charming, good looks, money, and obvious talent with racing, he has the full package. Sadly, Micah is too far out of my league, and I refuse to allow myself to believe that this could be anything more than Micah just wanting to slum it.

Micah: Well, then how about you come to a party? I'm hosting.

This time, I almost laughed out loud. Thankfully, my teacher didn't notice and neither did anyone else around me. I would never fit in at a party with Micah.

Me: Thanks...but no thanks. I am trying to get into another race anyway.

Maybe that will get him to stop asking. Soon enough, Micah will find some other girl to latch onto and he will forget all about me. A sudden drop of my stomach catches me off-guard. Why does that thought bother me so much? This is exactly why I can't continue—whatever this is between us—any longer. We are from two different worlds and neither of us have any business visiting the others realm.

Micah: Where?

Me: Where what?

I internally curse myself for asking. Why am I prolonging this further? I should block his number. Erase his name completely from my phone... but I can't force myself to do that yet.

Micah: Where is the race?

Anger consumes me. Is this why he's texting? Does he want another shot at beating me? Like hell I will give him that satisfaction again.

Me: Screw you! I need this race so don't even think about joining.

This time, I do block his number. The nerve of this guy thinking that he can swoop into my world and take something from me. I need these races to survive. He just needs a high.

I toss my phone into my backpack and then force myself to listen to the rest of the lecture. I know I sound crazy as hell, because honestly, I am so conflicted. Part of me can't help but fall for Micah's charm, but the other, more logical side of me, screams to ignore and forget about him. By the end of the day, I am so riled up, that I text Tank and beg him to sign me up for whatever races he can find. I need to earn some money and I am going to do it on my own.

Chapter Twelve

Micah

She blocked me!

I stare at my phone in disbelief as my message goes unread. I've never had a girl block me before. I'm used to be chased after and I've had to block a few crazy chicks before, but never has anyone not wanted to hear from me. Shaking my head, I feel a slap on my back as Talon sits down next to me.

"What's with the sad look?" he asks, as he places his tray down onto the lunch table. He sips on an iced coffee he purchased from the coffee bar.

"No sad look here," I reply, taking a large bite of my hamburger.

Our cafeteria isn't the typical high school cafeteria. No, ours is more like a food court you would see at a swanky mall. We have only the best food options available. At Royal Elite Academy, students are treated to the finest things that money can buy. We have state-of-the-art technology, college level sports complexes, and the body remains in pristine condition.

However, what makes this academy even more unique is the us; the Elites. Gabby, Talon, myself, and before he graduated—Ason. Everyone at school wants to be us and they go above and beyond to keep us happy. We are seen as royalty around here and I love being treated like a God.

While we walk the halls with everyone else, there is something vastly different about us. The power behind our names controls these halls with an iron fist. No one would ever dare cross us, because the stories they have heard of the gruesome acts from our fathers, have instilled such a wild fear in them, that they don't dare even breathe our way. At least, without being invited to first.

"Why are you staring at your phone?" Talon asks, around a bite of a chicken quesadilla.

Suddenly, I realize that I am still looking at the blocked message on the screen. I quickly shove my phone into the pocket of my khaki pants. "I was trying to remember some chicks name that I hooked up with last week. I'm going to have a party at the penthouse and wanted to invite her," I lie.

"You are having another party?" Talon asks, eyeing me carefully.

I hated lying to Talon, but we weren't as close as he was with Ason. All Talon wanted out of life was to be in the higher ranks with his father. Even when we were little kids, he was more mature than the rest of us.

"Yeah, a couple of sophomores are paying me to let them come for a while." While this isn't a complete lie, it's not one-hundred percent truth, either.

The Elites are paid to just show up to most parties, to advance popularity. Sometimes, some of our peers will pay us to let them show up for a while. They post pictures on their Instagram stories and then they leave. It's an easy way to make money...

My mind drifts back to Stella again. Why can't I stop thinking about her? I'm not sure if it's the fact that she ghosted me or doesn't find me appealing, but I feel this urge to find out. I know where she lives, and I may just have to pay her a little visit.

***

After school, I found myself driving down an unfamiliar road.

Instead of heading home, or back to Talon's house with him and Gabby, I decided to drive north- west to Stella's part of town. The southeast part of Savannah is where most of the wealthy live. I see the signs for Carver Heights, one of the crime capitals of Savannah, and instinctively lock the doors to my Range Rover. I felt uncomfortable and that put me in an even worse mood. If this is how I feel just driving through the area, how did Stella feel living here?

When I reach the trailer park, I turn in and drive slowly until I reach Stella's place. When I park, I spot Stella sitting rounding the corner of her trailer. When she locks eyes with me, there's a spark of anger that blazes through her features, then it turns to shock.

I get out of the vehicle and walk toward her.

"What are you doing here?" Stella asks, her voice laced with disdain.

"You blocked me," I respond, though my comment doesn't really answer her question.

Stella smiles, but it isn't from happiness. No this was a wicked, sinister smile that you see insane people give right before they kill someone in horror movies. I paused my strides and watched her carefully. "Most people would get the hint. I thought a rich boy like you would be smart enough to know that when a girl blocks you-- it means she doesn't want to talk to you," Stella sneers.

Oh, so she wants to be sarcastic. Well, two can play that game.

I smile right back at her, matching her evil stare. "Sorry, I wouldn't know. Girls don't block me—most are smart enough to know what a catch I am." I raise my brows at her and wink.

Stella huffs and I can see that I am getting on her nerves. "Or, maybe those girls are just too stupid to notice that you are an arrogant prick."

"Nah, I don't think that's it," I counter with a chuckle.

Releasing a heavy breath, Stella rubs at her temples. She's wearing a pair of cut-off blue jean shorts that show off her toned and tanned legs and her black tank-top hugs her frame nicely. My eyes travel the length of her body and Stella gasps as she watches me drink her in.

"Anyway, I have plans and I believe you need to get back to whatever criminal activity you have scheduled," she stated, trying to grate on my nerves.

I quickly close the space between us, and Stella is too surprised by my sudden actions to react. I stand towering over her, my body only inches from hers. She looks up at me with wide eyes and I lick my lips before talking. "Baby girl, you have no idea what I have planned," I say, running one finger along her arm. "Where are you going?" I ask.

Goosebumps rise from my touch, and I chuckle at her reaction. Stella can pretend like she hates me, but we both know that isn't the case. Her need to dislike me and everything that I represent is overshadowed by the desire I see radiating from her now.

Her lip quivers as she struggles to speak through a jagged breath. "You are right; and I don't care. Besides, I'm not telling you where I am going. Rich boys like you don't belong around here."

I highly doubt that's true. Stella's words may say she doesn't care, but her body and eyes are telling me otherwise.

"For some reason, I don't believe you," I begin, trailing my finger down her arm and then hooking it around the hem of her shorts. I touch the soft skin of her toned stomach and she sucks in a breath. "I think that you want to tell me where you are going." Leaning in closer, I breathe against her cheek, and she visibly shakes underneath my frame. "I also think that you want me to chase you."

This causes another reaction from Stella. She jumps back, forcing me to release my hold on her waist. Her cheeks are flushed, and her chest is rising and falling swiftly. "Why don't you just leave me alone?" she cries out, but her words are heavy and breathy.

I'm momentarily taken aback. This isn't at all how I expected her to react. I thought she would charge at me with another sassy comment, but this—raw emotion-- is not what I ever thought I would see from Stella.

"I was just messing around..." I begin, but Stella cuts me off.

"Thats your problem, Micah. You think this is all a game. A joke. Look around," she yells, waving her arms around. "This isn't a joke; this is my life. You get to come down here, act like a hero as you save the poor girl from the trailer park, then ride back to your kingdom on the nicer side of Savannah. I don't need your pity or your help. I can take care of myself—I've been doing it all of my life." She gasps, wiping away tears that are now pouring down her face. "There isn't anyone to look out for me, but me."

A sob escapes her as she finally breaks down. As I watch her crumble, I wonder if she's ever said any of those words aloud. A pain echoes through my chest as I watch this tough, strong, and independent girl break. Before I know what I am doing, I dart forward, rushing to her, and wrap my arms around her body. Pulling her in to me, I hold her tiny body while she cries. At first, she attempts to fight me off, but soon, she gives in and allows me to hold her. She grips my hands, clutching on to me like I'm her fucking life line. And right now, I want to be.

Her body molds to mine as if she were made just for me. A gasp tears through her, but she doesn't fight me anymore. The shift in her mood has me filled with so much emotion, I barely know how to contain myself. All of her pain is unleashing right now and damn it, I will be here to take it all on for her if she will let me.

"I will look out for you," I whisper into her ear.

Grabbing my hand, Stella pulls it up to her mouth and kisses my palm. A smile breaks through her tears and it's the most breathtaking thing I've ever seen in my life. My heart stills and my breathing stops. My eyes fall to her pouty lips. Right now, she doesn't need me to crash my lips to hers or to ravage her body. No, what Stella needs is consistency and to feel like someone cares for her.

"That could be nice," she says, her voice barely audible.

I have no doubt in my mind that those words were pure torture for her to say aloud. This is difficult for Stella; to trust someone else, but I will show her that I'm worth it. I squeeze her tighter and kiss her forehead. When she sighs, I know that she's calm.

I know that I can't take her pain away, but for this brief moment, I can give her something that she has never had before; support.

CHAPTER THIRTEEN

STELLA

I have no idea what in the hell is going on.

One minute, I was angry and ready to explode at the sight of Micah in front of my trailer. The next, I am wrapped up in his strong embrace, crying, and showing him a vulnerable side that I have fought so long to hide away from the rest of the world. I inhale his sweet scent and allow myself to drift away to some imaginary place where constant pain and fear doesn't exist.

After a few minutes, I squirm out of Micah's hold and take a step back. Now that the moment is over, embarrassment floods through me and I wish I could just be swept away by the wind. Not only did I cry in front of Micah, but I complained about how terrible my life is. He must think I am such a pain.

"I'm sorry," I mumble, struggling to compose myself. Wiping my tears away, I feel silly for allowing all of my emotions to break free. Though, I would be lying if I didn't admit that it was nice to have someone make me feel like I was safe.

Micah stares back at me, unmoving. "You have nothing to apologize for, Stella," he says. "How long have you been holding all of that in?" He's not being sarcastic or rude-- the question feels genuine.

"A long time." The words slip out and I instantly hate myself for being so honest. "Look, I appreciate your kindness, but what just happened there..."

"Why are you so damn stubborn?" Micah shouts.

His outburst causes me to flinch. Not because I am scared of him, but because of the emotion that was drawn out of him. Micah is elusive and gives off this vibe of being calm, cool, and collected. However, there is something deep inside of him that cares. That wants to be a better person.

I go to open my mouth, but for once in my life, I am speechless.

"I can help you," Micah says so quietly, I barely hear him.

"I don't need help," I reply, just as quietly.

Before I know what is happening, Micah grabs my face and crashes his lips against mine. The kiss starts angry and feral, but soon moves to sensual and sweet as his body relaxes and his hands slide down to my waist. We deepen the kiss as my hands fall to his chest. My fingers trace the outline of his abs and I loathe myself for how easily it is to fall into him like this.

When we finally pull apart, our eyes lock and there is this undeniable attraction that keeps us drawn to one another.

"I'm sorry, but I had to kiss you. I needed to shut you up," Micah says, and then I watch as his face squints and he shakes his head from frustration. "Fuck, that's not what I meant," he roars out.

"What did you mean, Micah? This is all getting to be too much. You at the race, and now showing back up to my place twice. What do you want?" I ask, exhausted by this game we seem to be playing.

Micah runs a hand roughly through his hair and I watch in awe as the late evening sun begins to reflect off his light hair. "What I want is-- you," Micah states with so much passion, I feel it all of the way down to my toes. "I've never felt like this before," he rushes out, running a hair wildly through his hair. "For a moment, you gave in and let me take that pain away.

Then, that storm inside of you rushed to the surface and you went all wild and crazy again," he huffs, shaking his head.

His words strike me like a lightning bolt. Maybe I didn't hear him correctly. Maybe he is confused about what he is saying. Guys like Micah don't want girls like me.

"Micah, that kiss was—amazing—but this doesn't make sense. We wouldn't make sense," I say, pointing between the two of us.

I'm arguing against the idea of us, but there is a part of my mind that is at war with myself. Would it be so terrible for Micah to fall for a girl from the wrong side of town? Would it be wrong for two people from two different worlds to fall for each other? I don't have the answers, but this need that I have to hear Micah out is overtaking all of my senses.

A sly grin appears over his face though, and I am captivated once again by his good looks. "That kiss was pretty damn great," he smirks. "Why do you care about what makes sense? Ever since I met you, I can't get you out of my mind. Look, I'm not the type of guy who has ever really cared about other people. Before I met you, I wouldn't have given anyone back their money. My family values money more than most things in life. I didn't even hesitate to help you out, though. And then, I was worried about you. Me, a fucking mafia knights' heir, was worried sick about you. I don't know what any of this means or what is going to happen, but all I do know is that I can't get you out of my head and I can't leave you alone," he roars.

I'm lost as I struggle to comprehend his words. No one has ever been so honest with me before. Most guys intentions with me are to just sleep with me or beat me in races. No one has ever cared enough to help me out financially or to worry about my safety. There's something about Micah wanting to be that person in my life that I find absolutely endearing. But I know not to get too attached to that feeling. Guys like Micah don't stay. They don't stick around after they make you fall in love with them. I refuse to end up like my mom; pregnant by a man who promised the world, but left once everything became too real.

"Micah, I know this is exciting, but we are so different," I argue again.

Tears prick my eyes again, but this time it's for an entirely different reason. I want to give in and be happy. I want to pretend like I live in a world where I can fall in love with Micah and that everything will work out for us. I could get lost in that fantasy and that is very dangerous for a girl like me.

Grabbing me by the shoulders, Micah forces me to look at him again. "Why are you fighting this so hard? Why can't you just see where this goes? We both have a lot to lose if this ends up badly, but we also both have a lot to gain, too," he tells me.

I go to open my mouth, but I quickly snap it shut.

I'm exhausted—both mentally and physically. I am so tired of fighting. For once, I just want to fall down the rabbit hole and get lost in the magic of love and safety and happiness.

Even if it won't last forever.

"Ok," I say, with a heavy sigh.

Micah's eyes grow wide, and he cocks his head to the side. "Ok?" he questions.

Nodding my head, I offer a slight smile. "Ok, you win for now," I say.

His face brightens with a wide smile, and I can't help but giggle at his reaction. "So, does this mean you will stop being so damn stubborn and unblock me?" he asks, pulling me in for a hug.

Even though I've fought him so hard, I give in and hug him back. "I can't promise that I won't still be stubborn, but I'll unblock you-- for now," I say, with a smirk.

Micah's arms tighten around me, and I can't help but snuggle further into his hold. There is something about having his strong arms wrapped around me that makes me giddy and smile. I can't remember the last time I've smiled so much and so genuinely in all of my life.

"Well, I'll get you to give in eventually," he teases.

Unfortunately, I think he is right.

His hold loosens and as he releases me, I feel that shield of comfort and safety slowly fade away. Part of me wants to jump right back into his arms again.

"Now," he begins, taking my hand, "Where are we going?"

That stupid smile that appears whenever he's around, is still glued to my face and I hate how silly I must look. "I have a race tonight. Tank called me after school."

I usually don't race on school nights, but I'm desperate. After Lucas added interest to my late payments for rent, I don't really have a choice. I need the money and I need it now.

Micah watches my face for a moment, and thankfully, he doesn't ask me any prying questions.

"Alright, let's go get your bike and go win a race," Micah says, and my heart leaps in my chest.

Chapter Fourteen

Micah

"Oh, shit. You live here?"

After we picked up Stella's bike, I drove us out to my house so I could talk with Talon and Gabby quickly. Pulling up to our compound, I watch as Stella leans forward in my SUV and gawks at the expansive property beyond the gates blocking out the rest of the world.

"Yeah," I say.

I've never cared about what other people think about where I live. Most of the people I know live in multi-million-dollar homes, but for some reason, I feel guilty as I watch Stella stare at my home. She lives in a dump, and this must seem like an entirely different world.

"How rich are you?" she asks, but her voice is low and I wonder if I was meant to her the question.

I don't bother to answer and continue up the steep drive. Parking, we get out of my SUV and I spot Talon and Gabby's cars. I had texted them earlier to meet me here. I wanted to talk to them about Stella and have them get eyes on that loser, Lucas. Stella is in some deep shit and regardless if she likes it or not, I'm going to help her out with this issue.

"This is my dad's money. I have to earn my way through life. Sort of like you," I tell her.

"But you already have so much. Will you..." she stops, un- sure of how to ask her question.

I used to get pissed when people would bring up my family and the mafia, but with Stella, it's just different.

***

Stepping into the house, Stella's eyes roam all over the foyer. She marvels at the artwork and family portraits lining the walls. Down the hall, I hear music and voices and know that Talon and Gabby are probably in the den where we have a pool table and bar. Taking Stella's hand, I surprise both of us as I lead her down the hallway.

When we reach the doorway, I see Talon leaning over the pool table, about to take a shot of the blue 8 ball. Gabby smirks next to him, holding her pool stick at her side. When she sees me, she smiles and nods. Stella and I walk into the room and Talon stands, stiffening at our approach. Sometimes, I wish he would lighten up a little. Even Ason finally relaxed a little over the last year.

"You ready to talk?" Talon asks, placing his pool stick across the blue lining of the table.

"Yeah," I say, releasing my hand from Stella's.

I hate how my stomach drops when I release her hand. I can tell that she feels the same way, too, because there's a sudden sadness that comes over her when I step back.

"Stella, stay in here with Gabby. I will be right back," I tell her, offering a small smile.

"Where are you going?" she asks me nervously.

"I just need to talk to Talon for a minute. You will be fine, Gabby won't bite," I chuckle, though, I'm not sure how true those words really are.

"I only bite a little," Gabby adds in, chomping her teeth.

Stella laughs a little, but I can tell that she is scared shitless. I nod to Talon, and we walk out of the den and down toward the dining room where I can close the French doors to hide our voices. Once inside the room, I spin around and start talking. I don't want to leave Stella alone with Gabby for too long.

"I've got a problem and I need for you to help me take care of it," I rush out.

Talon stands, his hands stuffed into the pockets of his designer jeans and a stern look across his features.

"What kind of shit did you get yourself in now?" he asks, giving me that disapproving look I have become so familiar with.

I tame down my anger and restrain from lashing out against him. Instead, I take a deep breath and focus.

"It's not for me. Stella needs our help. Her landlord is giving her problems and she has no one to help her out. He's harassing her and asking her to pay more than she can afford on her rent. I want to send a few guys to check him out and possibly scare him..." I let my words hang in the air.

Both Talon and I know that there is more hidden in what I'm saying. We don't just calmly talk to people. We fuck them up. Threaten them. Make them disappear.

"Is she worth it? Getting us involved?" Talon asks me.

Is she worth it?

I have been fighting my feelings for Stella, but to me, she is worth it. I've been chasing highs and rushes all of my life. Though, nothing has ever given me the adrenaline rush that I get when I'm with Stella. Being around her makes me feel wild and protective. I get this strange inner strength and an insane urge to do right by her. I will do whatever I can to help her and make sure that she is safe and taken care of.

Nodding, I stare at Talon so that he can see how seriously I am. "Yeah, man. She is worth it. And... I may be the first person in her life to ever show her that she's worth more than being the girl she thinks that she is," I say boldly.

Talon's eyes widen in surprise at my admission, but he doesn't say anything. Walking toward me, he places a hand on my shoulder and shocks the hell out of me when he smiles. "I never thought I would see the day," he chuckles, a sly smirk on his face.

Smacking his hand off of my shoulder, I narrow my eyes. "What day? What the fuck are you talking about?" I ask.

I don't like how amused Talon is right now and something tells me he is about to get on my last damn nerve, which happens to be his favorite hobby.

A spark ignites in his eyes, and he steps away from me. "Micah, you have been one of the most selfish, reckless, and infuriating people I have ever met. I swear, I never thought I'd see the day when you cared about someone other than yourself," he laughs.

Anger flows through me and I want to punch him right in the nose. "What are you talking about?" I roar out. I should keep my voice low as to now scare Stella, but I can't help myself. "I care about you, Ason, Gabby, and our family."

I hate talking about feelings and all that cheesy bullshit, but right now, I can't help myself.

"I'm not talking about the family. Micah, I know that you are loyal to the family and all of us," he states, waving his hand around, "but I'm talking about someone outside of our family. Being fierce and wild has always been your thing--what you are known for. This is different, though. You care about this girl and that means a lot to me. So, if she is special enough to make that cold heart of yours thaw a little, then I will make sure we take care of her like our own."

I'm in shock. I keep my face blank and try to hide the range of emotions that are coursing through me right now. Shrugging my shoulders, I motion for the door. "Look, I gotta get back to Stella. I will text you all later with more details."

Talon doesn't look my way, instead he moves over to the small bar against the wall. He pours himself a glass of aged bourbon and takes a sip. I watch him carefully and sense him trailing my movements, even though he isn't directly looking at me.

"I will wait for instructions," he says, wincing as he takes another large sip of his drink.

"Thanks," I mumble, before I leave the room and step out into the dimly lit hallway.

"What was that about?" I hear from being me.

Spinning on my hell, I see Stella standing behind her, her hands resting on her hips and a glare on her beautiful face. Gabby comes running into the hallway, shooting daggers our way.

"Going to the bathroom my ass," Gabby hisses.

Shrugging her shoulders, Stella continues to stare my way. "Sorry, I got lost," she says, though she never looks back to Gabby.

Throwing her hands up in the air, Gabby shrieks. "Go figure, Micah would find the sassiest and most stubborn woman to fall for. She's all yours," Gabby says, winking at me before retreating back the way she came from.

That one little movement had my heart leaping in my chest. Gabby approved of Stella and like it or not, Stella was now in my world.

Clearing her throat, Stella pokes me in the chest. My eyes tear back to her, and I can't help but smile. She turns me on when she's pissed and good for me, this girl is always fucking pissed. "You said you wouldn't be gone long. What's going on?" Stella asks.

Grabbing her by the arm, I pull her further down the hallway until we reach the garage. I open the door and pull her inside the massive, four car garage. Stella's anger instantly dissolves once she sees the sleek Jaguar and BMW SUV sitting in front of her.

Spinning her around, I force Stella to look at me, but her eyes bounce around at the cars and for some strange reason, I'm jealous of these material objects.

"Look, I had to talk with Talon about something. You can't just go roaming around my house by yourself," I begin.

Stella's eyes widen and for a brief moment, I think that she is going to hit me. "Why not?"

Damn, this woman is so stubborn.

"Look," I start, crowding her space and blocking her from looking anywhere else but me, "You know that my world is...complicated. I will take care of you, but you have to trust me and let me tell you everything when the time is right."

My breath stills and I pray to the God above that she will listen to me. Bringing Stella into my world won't be easy. She's used to danger and destruction, but what I live in is far worse than the nightmares I'm sure that she's imagined.

Stella goes to open her mouth, but then quickly clamps it shut. I finally release the breath I was holding and relax a little.

"So, are these all of your cars?" she asks, completely changing the subject.

A smile creeps over my face and I shake my head. "Mostly, they are my parents, but I can drive them if I want," I say, moving over to rub my hand along the black paint of the new Jaguar.

Stella follows me and I watch as her hips sway when she moves. My dick jumps to life, and I imagine bending her over one of these cars and fucking her until she's screaming my name. She is careful not to touch the car, but admires it from a close distance.

"Cars like these are sexy. So, where are your parents?" she asks me.

"Do you really want to talk about my parents right now?" I ask, gulping as I watch her hungry eyes stare back at me.

I know that she can see my hard-on growing in my jeans. Her eyes trail down my body and she smirks when she sees the affect that she is having on me.

"Not really," Stella admits. She traces one finger along the paint of the Jaguar, and I find myself craving to feel her touch again.

Moving toward her, I tower over her small frame, and I swear, I can feel her heart beating rapidly. "Well, my parents in Las Vegas taking care of business. They won't be home until sometime next week," I tell her.

It's strange how Stella has this power over me. She can make me share things—personal things—about myself that I wouldn't dare share with anyone outside of my family. I fucking love and hate the power she seems to have over me.

Damn, I'm in trouble.

"Huh." Stella slumps her shoulders.

"What?" I ask, oddly interested.

"It's just funny how different and similar our lives are," she notes, moving to the other side of the car.

"What do you mean?" I dare to ask.

She contemplates this for a moment before responding. "Well, both of our parents leave us alone, like a lot. But, the biggest difference is that you know that regardless of when your parents come back—and they will—you will be taken care. Bills aren't on your priority list. For me, the weight of the world falls on my shoulders every second of every day."

Stella looks almost shocked that those words came out of her own mouth. She let her walls fall and I know that she hates herself right now. Stella is strong and never lets people see her afraid, but with me, she is letting me have a glimpse at what life is like for her. And this is why I'm taking a huge leap of faith and letting her into my life. Stella needs me and damn it, I need her, too.

Before I know what I am doing, I rush around the car and stand so close to her, that I know that she can feel my breath against her skin. Her eyes meet mine and she bites her lip.

Fucking. Bites. Her. Lip.

Leaning down, I lose all sense of composure when I crash my lips against hers. My body moves on its own accord, as though I'm having some type of out of body experience, but this feels too good to be any type of dream.

When Stella's hands being massaging my head, pulling and tugging at my hair, I can't help but push into her body, forcing both of us to fall on top of the Jaguar.

Damn, if I let myself, I could lose myself with that girl. And, I just might.

Chapter Fifteen

Stella

I'm having an out of body experience.

Micah Lee is on top of me, his very large erection pressing into my thigh as his tongue invades my mouth. We are nothing more than hands and kisses and I can't think straight. I've been kissed before, but nothing like this. And something tells me that I will never find another kiss that makes me feel so—alive—like this ever again.

I moan, allowing my body to be mold into this overly expensive car beneath me. Nothing about this seems real. I'm in a house that costs more than all of the trailers in the trailer park, sitting on a car that I will never be able to afford, and being kissed by the son of a mafia king.

As much as I know this won't last, I can't help but want this to never end. There's a nagging inside of me begging and pleading to find a way to keep this feeling. To keep Micah.

Suddenly, Micah's phone buzzes in his pocket and we both still. Our eyes lock and I hate that the moment is over.

Smiling, I glance down to his pocket. "You should probably get that," I say.

Micah growls and pushes off of me. He adjusts himself before retrieving his phone.

"Yeah," he gruffly answers.

He nods as he listens to the person on the other line. I busy myself fixing my hair and adjusting my clothes back in place. My heart is still racing like a wild horse, but I try and act calm, cool, and collected.

After another minute, Micah ends the call and releases a heavy breath. The air around us has shifted once again and the lust that hung heavy, threatening to suffocate me, has lifted. Now, a strange vibe floats around us.

"That was Tank. He said we need to get to the race soon or you won't have your spot," he tells me.

Fuck.

I had almost forgotten about the race. Micah does that to me and it's another reason why this isn't good for me. It's dangerous for me to be distracted. I can't lose sight of my end goal; surviving.

"Ok, let's go," I say, smiling.

Micah surprises me when he takes my hand and walks us over to the door that would take us back inside the house. Instead, he pushes a button, and the garage door opens. I laugh at my own stupidity. I have only seen garages a handful of times in my life. I forgot that the doors opened. Just another thing separating us...

We hop in Micah's car and drive back to my side of town. The bright lights of Savannah slowly fade away as we approach my home. Manicured lawns and mansions just don't fit in with broken down buildings and crack whores walking the streets. A wave of embarrassment creeps over me, but I do my best to dissolve the emotion. This is my life. Micah understands that.

I grab my bike and Micah follows me to the warehouse district where the race is being held. Part of me fears for his vehicle, as car thieves are known to hang around these races, too.

"Are you not going to race?" I ask, as I realize we didn't even get his bike.

Shaking his head, Micah keeps his eyes glued to the road. "Nah, this race is for you, baby girl."

I keep my face blank, but inside, I am a giddy, excited girl that wants to smile brightly.

"I thought you liked racing? Remember, that's how we met," I joke.

In honesty, I'm trying to stop myself from wanting to jump him right here in this vehicle. Micah's too sexy for his own good and just one look from him can ignite me into a raging inferno of need.

"I do like racing, but you need this," he bites.

A sharp ache zaps me and I internally cringe. It's that feeling of pity I loathe and never want from anyone—especially from Micah.

"Don't do me any favors," I quip.

My fists dig into my legs as I fight the urge to cry. Micah and I shared one of the most life-altering kisses of my life, and now I am brought back to the cruel reality that I'm just this broken girl and he is a God among Gods.

A laugh escapes him, and I don't know whether to be surprised or pissed. "Stella, why do you always have to be so damn frustrating? I want you to race for you. I want to see you kick all of those guys assess and to win that money like a boss," he says.

My head shoots to face him and I get lost for a second as the lights from outside bounce all around him. In the darkness of the car, Micah's hand finds mine and all of the anger that had just consumed me, seems to evaporate. How can one man cause so many emotions to flood me all at once?

As far as I can tell, he's being genuine, so I do something that doesn't come easy for me. I keep my mouth shut and just enjoy the moment.

When we arrive, Tank yells for me to hurry and get registered. I barely have five minutes to get my name entered and to move to the starting line. Placing my helmet on my head, I drown out the world around me and try and focus only on the race. However, my body hums with need as I look to my right and spot Micah.

Micah waits away from the crowds, his arms crossed and a sly grin on his chiseled face as he leans against his Range Rover. The way he looks at me—like a predator stalking his prey—causes goosebumps to appear on my arms and a shiver to run down my spine. My body tingles at the thought of Micah kissing me again. I hear a gun shot, and I am brought back to the race again.

My opponents rev their engines as they launch forward. I had been so entranced by Micah; I missed the fucking start to the race! Pushing forward, I launch into the race. There are two bikes ahead of me, but I know these guys. Ricky, the guy to my right is a cocky bastard and will fall back soon enough. Jonah, to my left always gets a good start, but he can't handle his bike when it reaches max speed. I've seen him wipe out way too many times, when he hits a curve and his bike jerks. I focus ahead and spot the first sharp turn of the track. I lean to my right, allowing my bike to glide effortlessly on the track and I quickly pass Jonah. I right my bike again as a long stretch of the track approaches. I've raced this track a million times and know every bump, broken piece of pavement, and water filled holes. Avoiding a large puddle, I move to my right and soon enough the guy behind me hits the hole and his bike falls, sending him sliding across the pavement.

The moon over head is bright tonight and allows more light on the dimly lit track. This place is eerie and quiet, and I somehow find that comforting. I can hear the other bikes behind me, but I keep my focus ahead. Always focus on the finish line.

I've got one more turn and then it's a short, straight shot until I reach the finish line. The last turn comes with ease and once I see the crowd ahead, my heart beings to flutter with excitement. It isn't until I cross the line and see that I've won, that I slow my bike and head back toward Tank.

People cheer around me, but there's only one person I want to see. Searching the crowds of people, I spot Micah like a gleaming beckon of hope. Parking, I jump off my bike and rush toward him. Leaping into his arms, Micah grabs me and holds me tightly.

"You did it, baby girl," Micah whispers into my ear.

His voice is all I can hear as elation builds inside of me. He holds my ass up as my legs cross around his waist. I've never felt safer and more cared for than when I'm in his arms.

"This is amazing," I state, smiling into his neck.

Tank approaches and clears his throat. Micah doesn't release his hold on me, but spins me around so that I am now facing Tank. His large frame chuckles as he hands me an envelope filled with money.

Holding the cash in my hands, I sigh. I've won the race and can now pay Lucas so he will leave me the hell alone. Finally, something good is happening in my life.

***

Micah follows me back to the trailer so that I can park my bike.

The entire drive, I'm giddy and my body feels on fire. All I want to do is celebrate my victory with Micah and give Lucas his money.

When we arrive, I see that lights are on inside and a sick feeling builds in my stomach. Slowing, I move my bike to the back and when I round the corner, Micah is already out of his SUV. He's typing something into his phone, and I don't like the way his lips seem to snarl. He's fuming.

"Micah, maybe you should leave," I say, rushing up to him.

Placing my hands on his chest, I try to stop him, but he's too strong for me. He lets out a huff and its brash and deep, causing my stomach to drop. "No fucking way, baby girl," he snaps.

A shadow flashes across his face, and like a blur, he's zipping past me and racing toward the front door. I run after him, yelling his name, but I know that he isn't listening. He storms into the trailer, the front door almost falling off its hinges when he bursts through. When I reach him, he's panting and staring at a man who I don't recognize.

"Who the hell are you?" the man asks, rubbing scruff on his jaw.

For a second, I glance around, looking for signs of Lucas. Did he send somewhere here?

Micah cocks his head, and his angry, piercing eyes are shooting daggers at the stranger.

"Baby, I don't see anything," a hoarse voice calls, and my body stiffens at the sound.

Mom.

Of course, it's my mom. She typically shows up after a few months of being gone, some deadbeat boyfriend with her, and needing another fix.

"Mom, why are you here?" I ask, placing my hand on my hip.

Fear is long gone, but in its place is now annoyance. She would have to return tonight and destroy my elation of winning that race. My money is tucked away in Micah's SUV. I didn't want to drive with it and risk the wind blowing it away.

Gray, glossy eyes stare back at me as a slight smile appears over his tired face. "Hey, Stella," mom acknowledges.

"This the kid?" the guy asks, pointing to me.

I frown, trying to block out the years of trauma this woman has instilled in me. My head jerks toward the guy and I narrow my eyes. "Yes, I'm the kid. My name is Stella."

"Will someone tell me what in the hell is going on?" Micah asks, annoyance ringing in his tone.

"Micah, this is my mom, Debbie, and her boyfriend of the month," I sneer.

Mom dismisses the comment and I see her sniff and wipe at her nose. My guess, she's back on coke again. A nice upgrade from the meth she was doing with her last boyfriend. "Stella, I was hoping you had a little extra money you give me. Me and Ron," she says, pointing to the man I now know as Ron, "we got laid off of our jobs. A misunderstanding," she trails off, shaking her head.

It's always a misunderstanding with her. They probably got too high and didn't show up or stole from whatever loser had hired two junkies.

"Mom, you can't be serious right now. I haven't heard from you in months. Lucas has been giving me a really hard time about the rent," I stupidly try to reason with her, but I know she just can't understand.

She won't understand.

She never understands.

Waving her hand, she walks toward me from the hall, and I see her sway a little. She's probably drunk. "Stella, don't be ungrateful. I am your mom, you little shit," she shouts.

Ron chuckles next to her and I want to reach out and punch him in his stupid face.

"Ungrateful? What in the hell would I have to be grateful for?" I scream out, throwing my hands wildly all around me. "You disappear for months, leave me to be the adult around here, and then show up high with another loser asking me for money."

"Don't be disrespectful," mom chastises me. "How dare you talk to me like that. I let you live here!"

It's hilarious that she's trying to parent me. Wrong and hypocritical, but funny all the same.

Micah stiffens next to me, and his fists dig into his leg. Fury blazes in his features and I can tell that he is about to snap. Before I can comprehend what is truly going on, Micah opens his mouth and speaks. "Oh, I get it. You show up and expect your daughter, who has been paying rent and taking care of herself, to give you respect," Micah growls out, causing all eyes in the room to land on him.

"Watch it, kid," Ron says, stepping forward like he's going to intimidate us.

"You better watch it," Micah states, and I jerk back, unsure of what to do or say next.

The tension in the room is growing way too heavy. I hate that Micah is here and seeing the vile, disgraceful world that I come from. It's one thing for him to hear my stories, but it's a totally different story for him to see in the flesh, the woman that doesn't give two shits about me.

"Fuck is that supposed to mean?" Ron raises a fist and stands straighter.

Micah smiles and I see danger radiating from his eyes. "You have no idea who you are fucking talk to," Micah says, still having that sinister smile on his face. I am in awe, glued to the spot as I watch him unleash on Ron. "I own this fucking town. My father is part of the Antoni Mafia Family and if you ever so much as look at Stella, breathe in her direction, I will make sure they never find your body. Not even a piece of it," Micah says, low and gravely.

Ron gulps, but doesn't speak. My mom runs over and grabs his arm, looking between me and Micah.

"Stella, what kind of trouble have you gotten yourself into? Are you whoring around for the mafia now?" she asks.

Sad part is, she's fucking serious. That's how little my mom knows me. I'm not like her—nothing at all like the woman who birthed me.

"You'd love it if that were true, wouldn't you?" I ask. "I mean, to know that I'm no better than you would just make you feel less like a piece of shit for abandoning your daughter." Hot tears burn my eyes and I force them back. I can't let her see me break down.

Shrugging, my mom sniffs again and I can see that she is starting the downward spiral of withdrawal. "Stella, just give me a little money and then you can go back to whatever it is you were doing," she says, like she somehow has an idea of who I am.

Opening my mouth to speak, Micah turns to me, and I quickly close my lips. Micah reaches down and grabs my hand, squeezing and pulling me close to him. I find protection as I move to be closer to him. He's making a statement; it's us against them. Us against the world and I've never been so turned on and happy in my entire life.

"Nah, she Isn't like the trash that raised her. Now both of you listen to me right now. Don't you ever worry about Stella anymore. She will be taken care of by me. Stella is part of my world now and you don't need you," Micah snaps loudly.

My mom's glassy eyes raise, and she stares at me in disbelief. "Stella," she begins, but I don't allow her to finish.

Rolling my eyes, I allow Micah to lead me back to the door. I turn around and say, "Goodbye, mom."

And, I truly mean it.

This is goodbye because I never want to see her again.

This is goodbye because I finally have someone to care for me and keep me protected from scum like my mom.

And, goodbye because I am done with a life of constant hustling and struggling. Finally, I can live.

Chapter Sixteen

Micah

That wasn't at all what I was expecting.

Stella had been riding out her high from winning the race and then everything came tumbling down when her mom and some loser were at the trailer. The moment I saw Stella's mom and the complete look of hate and worry radiating in her eyes, I knew that I had to act. Stella is mine now and there isn't anything I won't do to help her.

When we first arrived at the trailer and we saw lights on inside, I texted Talon and told him to be ready if needed. Now, as I'm driving back to my house with Stella, I quickly type out a text for Talon and Gabby to meet me at the house.

"What about my bike?" Stella asks, her voice filling the silent car.

She bites her lip and worry creases her brows.

"Don't worry about your bike. I can get you a new one," I tell her, reaching for her hand.

Stella turns to look at me, and lights flash across her face. Fuck, she is so beautiful.

"I can't allow you to buy me a new bike. Micah, this is all so..." she hesitates, and her shoulders drop.

"So what?" I prompt.

Sighing, Stella tucks a lose strand of hair behind her ear. "I can't live with you, Micah. I can't tell you how much I appreciate you standing up for me tonight, but this is all happening so fast."

Gripping the steering wheel, I try to reign in my anger. Here we go again. Stella just can't accept the fact that I can and will take care of her. She tips her head as my jaw clenches.

"Why not?" I growl out. "Why do you always have to argue with me? I want to fucking take care of you. Let me do this for you, Stella. You deserve to have someone protect you. You are mine now and I won't let you go back to that trailer and be subjected to people who can't see how amazing you really are," I shout.

She's been neglected for far too long. The girl can't see love when it is staring her straight in the face.

Love.

Do I love Stella?

Hell yeah, I do.

I swear, from the moment I first met her, I knew there was something special about Stella. She isn't obsessed with my world, and she doesn't throw herself at guys with money. She argues with me. Pushes me to the fucking brink of insanity. Tempts me. And I love every second of it.

A frown pulls at Stella's face, but she doesn't say anything the rest of the car ride. When we finally pull into my house, I am relieved to see that the driveway is empty. Talon and Gabby are waiting on my call to show up.

Parking, I hop out of the SUV and when I round the corner, Stella is already out of the SUV. She stands in front of me, and I can't read the expression on her face.

"Stella."

A wide smile forms on her perfect lips and before I know what is happening, Stella leaps into my arms and her lips crash against mine. Grabbing her plump ass, I pull her to me as my tongue invades her mouth. Stella releases a moan, and I can barely contain my need for her. I walk us into the house, bumping into the door, as I refuse to release this goddess of a woman in my arms. I have no idea what has come over Stella, but I fucking love it.

Chapter Seventeen

Stella

Life has never been fair to me.

Hell, who am I kidding? Life has been a ruthless and evil bitch to me since the day that I was born.

I've lived in the wrong side of town. Gone without food and basic needs. Never felt love or acceptance. Well, that was until I met Micah.

There's an undeniable attraction between us and a raging inferno of need that grows whenever he is around. Tonight, listening to him stand up for me and then tell me that I was his—it almost broke me. The car ride back to his house was excruciatingly long as I waited to allow myself to finally give in to this man.

Wrapped in Micah's arms, he takes us upstairs and into a bedroom. When we fall onto a soft mattress, I can't help but moan when his lips trail down the sensitive spot on my neck. My body heats to scorching levels as Micah's hands roam over my breasts.

"Are you sure about this?" he asks breathlessly.

This man, who takes what he wants, and seems to own everyone around him, is asking me for consent. Nodding, I offer a slight smile as my hands fumble with the zipper on his jeans. Our passion is electric, and I've never wanted anyone like the way I want Micah. He's sweet and tender, but hungry as he takes control of my body.

I work his jeans off and he quickly removes my top and tosses it somewhere in the dark room. Soon enough, we are naked and panting, waiting to take the final step that we are both oh so craving.

"You are so beautiful," he whispers, as he slips between my legs.

My core is soaking wet and when Micah places one finger inside of me, he can feel just exactly how ready for him that I am.

"Micah," I say, placing my hands around his face. A sliver of moonlight filters into the room, providing me just enough light to make out Micah's glorious features. I swear, he takes my breath away as I watch his eyes trail over my face. "This thing between us—is it real?" I ask.

I don't think I am strong enough to resist Micah, especially if he says that what I imagine happening between us isn't real, but I also don't think that my heart could withstand that type of rejection from him, either.

Micah's face falls and he grips me tightly, pulling me closer to his body. He hoovers over top of me, taking control claiming me as his.

"Stella, this isn't just real—this is forever," Micah states, leaning down and kissing me with so much passion, my heart begins to race like a wild horse. "I love you. You are mine forever," he finishes, running one hand along my cheek.

He loves me!

I don't think I've ever been love before. At least, not until Micah found me.

"I love you, too," I say, tears filling my eyes.

Micah kisses me again, but this time it's slow and gentle. His hands fist my hair as he positions himself between my legs. His erection is right at my needy entrance and my hips come alive as they thrust toward him. A low chuckles escapes Micah as he sees just how needy I am for him.

"Be patient, baby girl," he huffs. "I'm going to take care of you," he states, kissing me.

I can feel that there is more in his words and that causes my heart to swell. I smile in spite of myself and then allow Micah to finally settle inside of me. At first, he moves slowly, allowing me to take him all in. I gasp when he enters me as the feeling of him stretching me completely is both painful and oh so amazing.

"Are you ok?" he asks me, stilling for a brief second.

Nodding, I can't help but smile again. Damn, he's going to think I am some giddy girl. "Yes, you feel so good," I moan.

My hands grip his strong shoulders as he begins a nice pace, but once he gets started, he moves fast and hard and I love every fucking thing about this. We are becoming one entity and I know that no matter what happens now, there is no going back.

There will never be anything but Micah for me now.

My climax builds and I dig my fingers so hard in his shoulders, I worry I may make him bleed. We climb higher and higher until we are both soaring on an unbelievable high. As I scream his name, riding out my orgasm, it's not long until Micah collapses on top of me, roaring out my name like a wild animal.

Panting, we both turn to one another, watching the other come down and settle back into reality. I've had sex with other guys before, but nothing has ever felt so right before. There isn't that awkward moment where you feel like you should say something to break the silence. The need to find my clothes and rush home isn't hanging over me.

No.

Instead, Micah pulls me into him, and I snuggle into his side. When his arm wraps around me, I sigh and allow myself to close my eyes. Pulling the cover up higher, I decide to rest, but Micah has other plans.

"What are you doing?" he asks me, slipping the cover down and exposing my bare breasts again.

"Ugh, I was trying to get comfortable..." I retort, rolling my eyes, in spite of the smile forming over my lips.

Shaking his head, Micah begins massaging my breast as he continues to pull the sheet down my body. "I haven't finished with you yet," he smirks, leaning down and placing his warm lips on my nipple. He begins sucking and kneading my breasts, a dangerous combination that is making me wet once again.

"That feels so good," I sigh, enjoying his touch.

I'm vulnerable and exposed right now; something I never thought I would feel with another person. Only Ally has ever known my secrets and fears, but now Micah doesn't just know them. He owns them. Micah took my heart and soul and now, he's made me feel alive and free.

Micah rolls back on top of me and just like that, he's inside of me once again and we go for round two of the best sex of my life.

***

The next morning, we go for round three while in the shower.

Micah hands me a cup of steaming hot coffee as we sit on his back porch, watching the early sun brighten the sky.

"Wow, I can't believe you really live here," I admire, taking the coffee.

The brick patio expands the entire length of the back of the house. French doors are open wide, allowing the outside to blend with the indoors. We sit on black iron chairs that face the back yard. Large Weeping Willow trees line a small pond where a few ducks swim along the surface of the water. The atmosphere here has a calmness that can't be found where I live.

Micah's jaw tenses and he doesn't say anything. I decide to ignore the look for now. He sips his coffee, staring out into the yard.

"I am going to call Lucas and let him know I have the money," I say.

"Let me handle that," Micah states.

Shaking my head, I place my coffee mug down on the black iron table in front of us. "No, I have to handle this. Besides, I need to go to the trailer..."

"The hell you do. I told you, you aren't going back there." Micah is tense and fuming now.

"Micah, my mom is probably gone by now. When she didn't get money, she had no more use to be there. I will be fine. Besides where in the hell am I going to live? I have to go to school on Monday and Ally will be worried," I explain.

Shit. That reminds me, I need to call Ally later and fill her in on everything that has been going on.

Micah stands and runs a hand roughly through his hair. A deep, dark chuckle rumbles through his chest. "You still don't get it, Stella," he says, through gritted teeth. "I want you here with me. I can protect you. I can provide a better life for you," he says, his wild, stormy eyes gazing right at me.

"Micah, I want to be with you, but we are seniors in high school. What you are saying is—crazy!" I shout, standing and throwing my arms up in the air.

A slight breeze filters through the patio and provides a much-needed reprieve from the steamy humidity of Georgia. Micah moves in on me, his mouth dangerously close to mine. When he is this close to me, my body reacts as if I can't control it. My heart leaps in my chest and I can feel arousal starting to take over. There is something so incredibly sexy about Micah when is angry and demanding. Maybe it's the possessiveness shining from his eyes. Whatever it is, has a hold on me and won't let go.

"Of course, it's crazy!" Micah roars. His warm breath is like a caress to my cheek, and I stand my ground while he fumes hoovering over me. "But, you know what else is crazy? Two completely different people falling for one another. A guy from the mafia finding a girl tougher than he is. A girl so strong and independent, she can take on the entire world by herself." He takes my hand and forces me to look at him. When our eyes lock, the world around us goes silent and It's like we are the only two people in the entire world. "We graduate in a few months. You can live at the penthouse; I know that my parents won't care. As long as you are safe, they will understand. I won't let you go back to that trailer. I won't let you be taunted and harassed by guys like Lucas ever again. I swear to everything in my fucking life that if Lucas or anyone else ever bothers you, I will kill them all with my bare hands."

I see the promise in his eyes and know without a doubt that Micah would do anything for me—even kill. He's right, though. While two teenagers planning a life together might sound insane to most people, we have gone through more than others could possibly imagine. Being with Micah is all I want and maybe, just maybe, it's a real possibility for me.

Biting my lip, I reach up and kiss him on his lips. "Let me think about it."

Micah muses and kisses me back. "I knew you wouldn't make this easy," he laughs.

"I never do." While I have every intention of being with Micah, I have to keep him on his toes. Our relationship isn't easy. We fight. Drive one another crazy. But we love harder and stronger. Together, we can take on the world.

Chapter Eighteen

Micah

I've chased the unobtainable all of my life.

Highs that exceeded the last.

Risks that would even terrify the bravest souls on Earth.

But Stella—she is something that I've chased and achieved.

The golden ticket.

The treasure that made me rich in happiness.

Watching her now, so brave as she sits in front of me, I catch myself practically ogling over her. She sees me watching her and she smiles, brightening the entire world.

"Yes, Lucas. I have it all," she says, rolling her eyes.

It takes every ounce of me not to rip that phone right out of her hands. Though, I know that what I have planned for Lucas later will make him think twice before he ever disrespects my woman again.

Stella nods, listening and at times, closing her eyes in frustration. When she's finally finished, she throws her phone down on the outdoor sofa and falls back into her chair.

"He's such an asshole," she cries out.

I instantly move to her side, almost begging her to let me take care of him. If this were any other situation, I wouldn't care what she thought. However, Stella needs me to back off. Well, as much as I possibly can.

"What happened?" I ask, biting my lip so hard, I can taste blood in my mouth.

I want to scream and throw shit, but I don't. I rein in my anger with the promise of shedding blood later.

Shaking her head, Stella pinches the bridge of her nose. "He added more interest to what I owe."

Her words have me seeing red. Reaching into my pocket, I send a text for Gabby and Talon to meet me.

"What are you doing?" Stella asks me with wary eyes.

She knows and I don't care.

Leaning down, I place a soft kiss to her forehead. "I have to go," I tell her.

"Micah, wait!" Stella calls, grabbing my arm and halting my steps.

I spin around, seeing the worry creasing her brow. "What?" I growl out.

She winces at the snap of my tone, but she quicky recovers. "Micah, don't go do anything stupid," she warns.

"I won't. I'm just going to stake out the place while you take the money to Lucas. If anything goes down, I will be there," I tell her.

I can see in her features that she doesn't like the idea, but she also knows there is no arguing with me now.

"Fine," she huffs. "Just let me handle this. If Lucas does anything stupid, then you can step in," she agrees.

A smile breaks out on my face, and I pull Stella into my arms. She thinks she has won right now, but we both know, I fucking won the moment Stella stepped into my life.

Chapter Nineteen

Stella

Ally picks me up at the end of Micah's long driveway.

"Holy shit. This is where you live now?" Ally whistles, straining her neck to see further up the driveway.

I close the door and settle into the seat. "I don't live here," I say, but I don't sound convincing.

Ally shakes her head, and we begin driving away from Micah's house. At first, we ride in silence. Only the sound of the radio playing lightly in the distance. After a while, Ally finally breaks the silence. "So, what exactly are you doing, Stella?" she questions me.

"What do you mean?" I ask.

Gripping the steering wheel tighter, Ally looks annoyed. "Stella, don't play dumb with me. You all of a sudden disappeared. You haven't been at your trailer. You haven't been calling and texting me. You meet this rich guy and it's like you have fallen off the face of the earth," she deadpans.

I grit my teeth. "It's not like that at all. Micah loves me and he wants to protect me. He's offering me a way out of the hell I've been living in," I admit.

Ally doesn't say anything else and when we reach his trailer, I feel a lump forming in my stomach. Being back here is unsettling. I hop out of the car and run the money up to the door. Lucas opens before I can even knock on the old door.

"Well, looks like you came through," he says, eyeing me carefully.

"I have it all," I say, venom dripping from my words.

I absolutely hate Lucas. He is nothing more than a waste of space and I can't wait until I never have to see him again.

He takes the envelope I hand him and counts every single dollar. Of course, he would think I was trying to skimp on paying him. He doesn't trust anybody.

"What about my added interest?" he asks.

Huffing, I fold my arms across my chest. Being so close to Lucas makes me feel dirty and exposed. "I'm not paying you anymore, Lucas. I don't owe you anything anymore. I'm never coming back here again," I tell him, holding my head up high.

Lucas chuckles, spittle flying out of his mouth. "That's what you think. Girl, you came from trash and will always be trash. You belong here and that pretty rich boy will get tired of your pussy soon enough," he states.

I want to vomit at his words. He is such a vile creature, and he is just another reason why I should allow Micah to help me out. I don't want this life. I have to rise out of here and be brave.

"Whatever, Lucas. You have your money, goodbye," I state, spinning on my heel to leave.

I rush off his porch and race toward Ally's waiting car. When I open the passenger door, Lucas calls out my name. "I will collect what is owed to me," he roars out.

I slam the car door and shout for Ally to drive. Tears sting my eyes, but I refuse to cry. I've shed enough tears over this place and the people in it. It's time for me to start a new journey with Micah.

***

Over the next few weeks, life has completely changed for me.

Micah talked with his parents, and they agreed to let me move into the penthouse. However, I refused to do it unless

I could contribute finally in some way. Racing couldn't be my only source of income anymore, so I got a job waiting tables at a restaurant in the hotel. Micah even gave me one of his cars; a pearl white BMW to drive to school. Even Ally has come to terms with my new life and loves hanging out with me at the penthouse after school. Thankfully, I haven't heard from my mom again, but I know that I need to go back to the trailer one last time and get a few personal items that I want to keep. Lucas is already looking for a new tenant to rent it out, so I need to get over there soon or my stuff will be thrown away.

It's Friday after school and I get a text from Ally.

Ally: Lucas is throwing all of the shit from your trailer out on the street. You better get over here and take what you still want.

Rolling my eyes, I release a heavy breath. I had wanted to wait until Micah could go with me, but I can't wait now. I'm sure the neighbors have already started picking through what Lucas has taken out of the trailer. I run toward the BMW in the student parking lot and race to the other side of Savannah. A place I had avoided like the plague—until now.

I should probably call Micah, but I'm too focused on driving like I'm in the Indy 500 to pause and call anyone. Besides, I won't be long.

When I roll up to the trailer, I already see people picking through my items. A few people scatter, but the rest ignore me.

"Hey, what the hell are you doing?" I shout at them.

Two girls who work at the strip club down the street run away, carrying handfuls of my clothes. Anger consumes me as I look at broken picture frames and dishes lining the street. Lucas literally just threw everything out. I move toward the trailer and once I'm inside, I gasp from shock.

Broken furniture and glass liters the dirty carpet. Graffiti is spray painted all over the walls and the stench of garbage almost makes me gag. The copy of Streetcar Named Desire is torn into a million tiny pieces on the kitchen counter and what little food I did have, is completely gone. Lucas allowed people to come in here and destroy the place.

Moving toward my bedroom, I stare at my small desk where the few personal items I cared about are shattered.

"Look who decided to slum it," a nasty voice says from behind me.

Spinning, I spot Lucas standing behind me. Panic rises inside of me as I see the hatred in his eyes.

"Why did you do this?" I cry out. "I paid you, Lucas. Why did you have to destroy everything?"

Laughter fills the room as Lucas steps closer to me. His hot breath reeks of stale beer and sweat forms over his brows.

"Little bitches like you need to learn their lessons," he sneers, taking a hand and running it over my cheek.

I slap his hand away, disgusted by his proximity. "Don't touch me," I warn.

"Or what? You will sick your little gangster boyfriend on me? I've heard about the Antoni Mafia Family. Girl, you don't know what you've gotten yourself into," he mocks me.

"He will kill you," I state, through gritted teeth.

Raising his fist, I don't have time to react before his hand slaps me across the face. Pain sears my skin and I'm so stunned; I am almost immobile.

"It's time you learn a lesson, slut," Lucas shouts out.

I only have enough time to step back, before his fist comes flying toward me and everything goes black.

Chapter Twenty

Micah

"Where the fuck is she?"

Slamming my fist on the dashboard, rage takes over my body.

When Stella didn't call me after school today, I sent Gabby to the penthouse, but it was empty.

I've been calling her for the last hour, and she's not answers. This isn't like her, and I know that something is wrong.

"Did you all get into a fight?" Talon asks me.

He sits in the passenger seat, sending a message to Ason asking for help. When any of us get a feeling like something is wrong; we share it with each other. In our world, you always have to be prepared.

"No, man. I told you, things are good between us. Something has happened."

We drive from the hotel and casino and Gabby is following behind us. None of us have reached out to our parents yet. I need to handle this myself first. This is just another way that I can prove my worth to both the Antoni Mafia Family and to Stella.

My phone rings and I answer the call. Gabby's voice comes in loud through my car speakers. "Micah, security at your house and the hotel both said that they haven't seen Stella. Can you think of anywhere else she could be?" she asks.

I take a moment and wrack my brain. Her trailer comes to mind, but there is no way she would venture back to that place alone. She couldn't...

But, Stella is stubborn.

"I think I might know where she is. We need everyone to meet me at Stella's trailer," I shout.

I text in our group chat her address and then race to the last place I ever thought I would see again.

***

The moment we drive into the trailer park, I instantly know something is wrong.

A crowd of people block the street and I nearly run them all over on my way to find Stella.

"Is that smoke?" Talon asks, as he rolls down the window.

A heavy, gray fog rolls into the car and the odor of smoke burns my nostrils. Something is on fire around here and that thought has my nerves instantly going crazy.

"Move the fuck out of the way," I yell out my window, as I continue driving.

A girl runs from the opposite direction, her face stained with streaks of tears, and her sobs breaking through the noise around us.

"Help!" she cries, but no one pays her any attention.

Rolling to a stop, I hope out of my car and rush toward the girl. "What's going on?" I ask.

Gabby pulls up in her red Mercedes convertible and Ason is close behind her in a large, black truck.

Talon is at my side and grabs the girl around the shoulders to help calm her down. "Hey, tell us what happened."

"My friend...she's in there..." The girls' cries come out in waves and my stomach drops.

I have no doubt in my mind that this is Stella's friend, Ally. The way Stella has talked about her, I just sense it's her.

"Who is your friend?" I ask, dreading the answer I know is about to come.

"Stella. You are Micah," she states, knowing damn well who I am.

I don't waste any time answering her. Instead, I take off in a wild sprint as I shove my way through the crowds to get to Stella. Just as I dreaded, the smoke that we smelled earlier, is coming from Stella's trailer. Everyone stares at the blazing inferno, but when I scan the scene, I don't see Stella anywhere. My hand grips my phone as I dial Stella's number again. It's no use though. She doesn't respond.

Ason, Talon, and Gabby stand next to me, waiting for me to tell them what to do.

"I have to go in there and find her," I state.

Shaking his head, Ason is the first to respond. "I just called 9-1-1. Wait for the fire department to get here," he tells me.

I look to Ason. My eyes plead with him to understand. To not stop me when I do the unthinkable. Tearing into a mad dash, I race toward the blazing inferno that has taken over Stella's trailer. A heavy black smoke consumes me and my eyes sting as I struggle to keep them open. I see nothing but darkness around me and all I can think about is finding Stella.

"Stella," I yell out, but my lungs fill with smoke, and I begin coughing.

Dropping to my knees, I crawl down the narrow hallway on my way to her room. The tiny living room and kitchen are empty, so that only leaves me with a few more options. I still can't see, but as my hands feel around, I suddenly bump into something and my body stills.

A wet, sticky liquid coats my hand and I fight back to the urge to scream. It's blood.

"Stella," I croak out, feeing around until I touch her hand.

She doesn't move, but I know it's her. Moving to my knees, I grab her frail, limp body and lift her into my arms. It takes all of my energy to carry her through the smoke and out of the trailer. I go only by memory as I maneuver through the space.

Once I reach outside, I finally inhale fresh air and collapse onto the grass.

A fireman rushes to me, pulling a lifeless Stella from my arms. I go to protest, but he slaps a breathing mask on my face. I try to push him away, but my body is weak from the smoke and all I can do is sit in the grass and watch as the paramedics help the fireman place Stella inside of an ambulance.

"Stella," I try to call out, but it's not use.

She can't hear me, and I am so far out of my body right now, that I know I'm a million miles away from her. Hot tears sting my eyes and as much as I know that I should wipe them away, I don't.

Ally is at my side, screaming and yelling, but I don't hear a word she says. In fact, I don't hear anything at all. I'm stunned. For the first time in my life, I was scared. Not just scared, but terrified to my very core. It's as though my body has become numb and lifeless. A sting cuts through my heart and it takes my final breath away.

Gabby moves in front of me, her arms waving around as she points between me and the ambulance. Still, I don't hear anything, and my body remains frozen in place. My mind is shouting for me to jump up and follow Stella, but I just can't. I've never felt this helpless before in my life. Firemen race around the trailer, their hoses spraying gallons of water on the blaze. Police bombard me with questions, but again, I don't hear them. At some point, I become nothing more than a permanent fixture on the lawn. Everyone just moves around me as they chaos builds and then quietly comes to an end.

An angry Gabby finally runs toward the ambulance and climbs inside. Every damn nerve in my body is screaming for me to follow Gabby. To check on Stella. She has to be ok.

I have no idea how long I sit in the grass, but at some point, the world around me has grown black and all that's left is me and Ason. The neighbors left once the paramedics and police did.

"Are you ready to go?" Ason finally asks.

My head slowly turns to face him and I swear, it's the first time I've moved since I came out of the trailer.

"I have to fix this," I say, through clenched teeth.

Ason nods, his knowing dark eyes staring back at me. Ever since he left for college, we haven't spent as much time together as we should. He's happy and in love and I finally get why he was willing to give up everything for Scarlette. When you meet someone who you can't ever life without, nothing and no one else matters.

"We will. You have us, but first, you have to go get your girl," Ason says.

There is a fierceness behind his words, and he knows that I'm going to do something that I won't ever be able to come back from. But I don't care.

First, I will make sure Stella is ok.

Then, I will kill Lucas.

***

"Please, I'm sorry."

As I stare down at the pathetic excuse for a man, my rage almost blinds me.

My pistol is shoved into his forehead as he kneels before me. Blood trickles down his face and Ason and Talon stand behind him, smug grins on their faces as they wipe Lucas's blood off their hands.

After Ason drove me to the hospital and I was promised that Stella would be ok, we left Scarlette there to watch over her while security and my parents showed up. Talon called our dads, and they were sure to get Doctor Ramirez to the hospital and then, brought us everything we needed to handle our situation with Lucas.

Each of our methods are different, but the end result is always the same. You fucking mess with ours, we kill you.

"You should have begged for Stella's forgiveness, but instead, you attacked her," I roar out.

Gabby turns from the door and smiles wickedly at me. She is a savage and fucking loves it when we get to bring Karma to assholes. Her glock is held up high, warning anyone within earshot that if they dare to intervene, they won't make it out alive, either.

"She owed me money. You have to understand that," Lucas attempts to plead with me.

Only, his words have triggered more anger inside of me. I slam my glock in his face, watching with pride as blood sprays all around me. Lucas cries out in pain and as he goes to fall over, Micah quickly kicks him back onto his knees.

"Stella paid you. But you're a greedy bastard and you thought you would keep harassing her. Well, you won't ever bother anyone ever again."

I motion for Micah and Ason to pick up Lucas and as they do, Lucas screams and begs for forgiveness, but it's too late. We carry him out of his trailer, the eyes of the trailer park on us, and shove him into the back of Ason's truck. We drive away from the trailer park for the very last time.

When we reach our property twenty-minutes later, we drive back to the first place that sparked something inside of me. It's not lost on me that I am about to do something that I watched my own father do when I was just a child.

"Are you sure about this? You know, man, there's no coming back from this. Once it's done, that becomes who you are," Ason says, from the driver's seat.

Micah and Gabby sit silently behind us. They know that your first kill is your choice and yours only. We all know what it means, and we have to make that decision with our own minds.

"I know what I am doing. It might not be the choice you would make, but it's what has to happen. Imagine if that had been Scarlette," I say, knowing that my words will resonate with him.

Ason loves Scarlette and they are going to get married. Even though he hates killing, I don't doubt for a second that he wouldn't do the unthinkable if it meant saving Scarlette.

"I'm not trying to talk you out of anything. I just want you to understand. I haven't been around much since I went to college. I've missed out on a lot and haven't been here for you guys like I should have. But, I'm here now," Ason says.

I don't fault him for going away for college. It's the decision he made and it's his journey that he had to take.

The truck rolls to a stop in front of the swamps. The sun has settled long ago and now only the stars shine down on us, watching us and waiting to make judgement. We get out of the truck and the sounds of frogs and owls ring through the night air. In the distance, I can see the glow of lights from our houses far, far away from this site.

Micah pulls Lucas out of the truck bed, and he's barely conscious. As he lay in front of me, his eyes look up to mine one last time. "What are you going to do to me?" he finally asks, his voice barely above a whisper.

"I'm not going to do anything to you. You are going to take a swim. Now, I can't speak for the gators, but I'm sure you will figure something out," I say, as his eyes go wide.

I kick his body and watch as it rolls into the water with a loud splash. It doesn't take long for the alligators to begin their frenzy. We stand back and wait until the sounds wash away and its only silence left.

As I turn to head back toward the truck, a sense of relief washes over me. After tonight, anyone who dares to fuck with Stella will know that their fate will be met at the bottom of an alligator infested swamp.

Chapter Twenty-one

Stella

I wake with a pounding headache and annoying beeping that won't seem to end.

Stirring, I slowly open my eyes, but they sting. It takes a second before I can fully open them and once I do, it's like I'm being blinded.

"Hey, be careful," a rough voice says.

My heart rate increases and I'm instantly alert and awake. Through the pain I feel, I turn and spot Micah standing beside me, but everything else is wrong.

White walls and machines surround me and when I look down, I realize I'm not in his bed, but in a hospital bed.

"Where am I?" I ask, but my voice is hoarse and my throat stings like I've swallowed a million tiny razors.

Taking my hand, Micah smiles at me and I see tears—real tears—pouring down his face. My stomach drops at the sight, and I suddenly grow worried.

"Where is everyone?" I ask, my voice breaking.

"We are right here, Stella," Gabby says from across the room.

Before me now stands, Gabby, Talon, Ason, Scarlette, Ally, and Micah's parents. Now I'm really freaking out.

"Stella, what do you remember about last night?" Micah asks, concern ringing in his tone.

I stare blankly at him and as I take him in, I begin to notice the bruises on his knuckles, the tear in his white t-shirt, and the cut on his upper lip. He's a complete wreck, but he's still sexy as hell.

My brain goes to think, but my head pounds again. Flashes of red and yellow flames cross my vision and then a sharp pain pierces my head. More tears spill out of my eyes, and I hate how scared I feel right now.

Micah sits beside me on the bed, pulling me in close to him. The movement hurts, but I don't care. I need his protection and the nearness of him right now.

"There was a fire at your trailer. You were inside and Micah saved you. But, the doctors said that you had been attacked. A few neighbors said they saw Lucas enter your trailer right after you did," Talon tells me.

Guilt consumes me as I remember going to get my stuff, but not feeling the need to call Micah. I should have known better. Lucas had been such an asshole about wanting more money, but I never thought he would do something like this. He tried to kill me!

"I'm so sorry," I sob into Micah's chest. "Please forgive me. I just wanted to get my things and then never have to see that place again."

"I saw Micah driving near your house and I told him that you were inside," Ally explains.

Everyone who I love is inside this room right now because of me. I'm filled with both happiness and immense regret for the poor decision I made. I'm relieved they are here, but this could have easily been a very different situation. As much as I hate to admit it, I need family. I need the love and protection of those around me. I need a team; a support like the Antoni Mafia. Sure, I'm independent and can take care of myself, but I have learned over the last few weeks that I don't have to. I can rely on those who care for me and I should.

A doctor walks in and everyone turns to stare. He nods and chuckles, his gray hair shining under the light. "It's nice to see you awake, Stella," he says. "I'm Doctor Ramirez, one of the Antoni Family personal doctors. I usually work out of my...office... but Micah insisted that I come to the hospital and personally see to it that you are taken care of. While you are very lucky to be alive, you did experience a nasty blow to the head which resulted in a minor concussion. Your lungs were full of smoke and you were severely dehydrated. We would like to keep you here another night for monitoring, and then I think you will be ok to go home," he explains, his warm eyes making me feel comforted.

"I didn't think any of this would happen. What about Lucas?" I ask, my lips trembling.

Just thinking about him causes severe anxiety to spike inside of me.

Doctor Ramirez's eyes flash to Micah and his dad. I notice how Micah's jaw ticks and Ason, Talon, and Gabby give one another knowing looks—like they are have some private conversation only they can understand.

"Baby girl, you never have to worry about Lucas again," Micah whispers into my ear.

My eyes shoot up to his and I see that he is pleading with me not to ask more questions. Unease creeps over me because I know what that means. Lucas is gone. Forever.

Micah's parents smile warmly at me and then after a few minutes, they leave the room and I see them talking to security officers outside of my room. Doctor Ramirez gives me more information and a nurse comes in to check my vitals and bring me some water.

After a while, everyone leaves but Micah. Once it's finally the two of us, I snuggle deeper into his side. "Micah, am I able to ask you about Lucas?"

I don't bother looking at him. I can feel his body grow tense at the mention of Lucas.

He closes his eyes and then slowly reopens them. Kissing the top of my head, he waits a few minutes before finally responding. "Stella, when I found you, I thought you were dead. I have never felt that scared and helpless before. I couldn't do anything once I got you outside. It was like my body just stopped working. When I finally came to, I rushed straight to the hospital after calling my dad and asking him to help by calling Doctor Ramirez. Once I knew you were going to be ok, a new type of fear took over me. I had to stop Lucas from ever hurting you again. I'm not proud of what I did, but I would do it again in a heartbeat if I knew it would mean you were safe," he says.

My heart beats wildly knowing that Micah did something terrible just to protect me. But, that is the world he lives in, right? And, the world I guess I now live in, too.

"I love you so much for saving me and being so worried about me, but the last thing I ever want is for you to harm anyone because of me." I can't bring myself to say murder—but we both know that's what he did.

Gritting his teeth, Micah shakes his head and lets out a heavy breath. "Stella, I would die for you. I would walk to the ends of the earth if I knew it would make you smile. You are my world and nothing else matters but you. I know you are new to my lifestyle, but in my world, we take care of our own. Our ways might not be moral or legal, but we send a message and I sent one last night and now the whole fucking world knows that if they mess with you, they mess with me and the Antoni Mafia Family."

All I can do is nod. I knew that once I accepted Micah's heart and soul, I accepted everything about him.

The good.

The bad.

The dangerous.

"So, what now?" I ask, sighing.

Holding me tightly, Micah chuckles lightly. "We get you the hell out of this place and back to your penthouse. You keep working and we finish high school in a few short months. We go to college, get married, and have lots of babies. We live the rest of our lives fucking happy together."

I can't help but smile at that. It might sound crazy to most people, but I know that our life together will be amazing. We might be young, but our love knows no boundaries. We have both seen and experienced more than most people twice our age. We had to grow up early because that's the hand we were dealt in life. I have no idea what our journey will look like, but as long as I have this wild, reckless boy by my side, I will be able to handle whatever life throws our way.

Together, we will love one another and survive because that's all we know how to do.

The End

About Author

M. A. Lee resides in a small Kentucky town and enjoys writing tales of romance that includes the bitter and sometimes ugly truth of love, angst, heartache, and desire that all come with falling in love.

Enjoy this story?

Leave a review on **Amazon-**

Find me on:

GoodReads-https://www.goodreads.com/author/show/18-422927.M_A_Lee?from_search=true

Connect with me on:

Facebook-https://www.facebook.com/profile.php?id=100-015891935024

BookBub-https://www.bookbub.com/authors/m-a-lee

Also By

Also Written by M. A. Lee
The Breaking Boundaries Series
<u>Breaking Boundaries</u>
<u>Breaking Through</u>
<u>Breaking Promises</u>
Breaking Trust

The Heavy Hitters Series
<u>Knock Out</u>
<u>Stone Cold</u>

A Christmas Anthology
<u>'Tis the Season</u>

<u>New Jersey Boy</u>
<u>Chasing Us</u>

A Savannah Mafia Romance
<u>Cruel Prince</u>
Cruel Warrior
Cruel King
Cruel Knight

<u>Multi-author collaborations</u>
that can be read as standalone novels.

The Raven Boys Series
Twin Flames
Burning Hearts

The Crimes of Passion Series
Faded

The Shady Oaks Series
Moonstruck

The Legacy Series
A Shot at Love
Running to You

A Rescue Me Series Novel
Falling for You
Blazing for You
Aiming for You

An Everyday Heroes World Novel

Taken

The Driven World Series Novel

Limitless
Rush

A Hero Club Novel

Cocky Professor

A Salvation Society Novel
Scorched